S0-ACP-417

"It's very simple, Chloe James. I intend to take you as my wife."

Chloe felt as though she'd been punched in the stomach, all the air leaching from her body, making her gasp. "What?"

"Not a real wife, you understand. This is about presenting the image of a family to the people. If I am meant to raise Aden as my own, my wife will be expected to treat him as her own. You want to stay, you want that role, so I am giving it to you."

"But…you want me to marry you?"

"I don't want you to marry me, I want to protect Aden and give the people what they expect, give them an image that will bring comfort."

Chloe felt as if her heart was trying to claw its way up her throat. Failing that, she was certain it would beat through her chest. She knew all about marriage. About the dynamic between a husband and wife. About what a man did when he saw a woman as his property.

SECRET HEIRS
of
POWERFUL MEN

Their command is about to be challenged!

Sheikh Sayid al Kadar and Alik Vasin might not be related by blood, but these brothers-in-arms forged an unbreakable bond in the line of duty.

They've fought for their countries, for their lives, but has that readied their hearts for what could be the biggest battle of them all?

Heir to a Desert Legacy

April 2013

Sheikh Sayid discovers that his brother is survived by a son, and he'll do anything to recover the true heir to the throne. Even if it means taking on the child's aunt; she's like a lioness who insists on fighting him every step of the way!

Heir to a Dark Inheritance

May 2013

When Alik's wayward past comes back to haunt him, he'll ensure that his young daughter will grow up with a childhood nothing like his own. But one woman is standing in his way, and there may be only one solution—to marry her!

Maisey Yates

HEIR TO A DESERT LEGACY

SECRET HEIRS
of
POWERFUL MEN

HARLEQUIN PRESENTS®

Recycling programs
for this product may
not exist in your area.

ISBN-13: 978-0-373-23903-0

HEIR TO A DESERT LEGACY

HARLEQUIN®
™ www.Harlequin.com

Printed in U.S.A.

All about the author...
Maisey Yates

MAISEY YATES knew she wanted to be a writer even before she knew what it was she wanted to write.

At her very first job she was fortunate enough to meet her very own tall, dark and handsome hero, who happened to be her boss, and promptly married him and started a family. It wasn't until she was pregnant with her second child that she found her very first Harlequin Presents® book in a local thrift store—by the time she'd reached the happily ever after, she had fallen in love. She devoured as many as she could get her hands on after that, and she knew that these were the books she wanted to write!

She started submitting, and nearly two years later, while pregnant with her third child, she received The Call from her editor. At the age of twenty three, she sold her first manuscript to the Harlequin Presents line, and she was very glad that the good news didn't send her into labor!

She still can't quite believe she's blessed enough to see her name on, not just any book, but on her favorite books.

Maisey lives with her supportive, handsome, wonderful, diaper-changing husband and three small children, across the street from her parents and the home she grew up in, in the wilds of southern Oregon. She enjoys the contrast of living in a place where you might wake up to find a bear on your back porch, then walk into the home office to write stories that take place in exotic, urban locales.

Other titles by Maisey Yates available in ebook:

Harlequin Presents®

For my readers. Without you, none of this is possible.

CHAPTER ONE

SAYID AL KADAR SCANNED the empty street and tugged the collar of his coat up, shielding the back of his neck from the raindrops that were threatening to infiltrate. The Portland drizzle was intolerable in his opinion.

Even in this more desirable part of the city, everything seemed locked together. Stone on the road, the walk, the buildings that stretched up into the sky. It all felt closed in. A glass-and-steel prison. It was no place for a man like him.

No place for the heir to the throne of Attar. And yet, according to every piece of data he'd gathered over the past twenty-four hours, this is where the heir to the throne of Attar was.

The moment he'd found the paperwork in his brother's secret vault, he'd been driven to find out if there was a chance that the heir had survived. Alik had confirmed not only the child's survival, but his whereabouts, in record time. Not that his friend's speed and efficiency should surprise Sayid at this point. Alik never failed.

Sayid shoved his hands into his pockets and crossed the street, just as a woman was approaching the same apartment building he was intent on.

He smiled at her, reaching for the kind of charm he'd buried long ago, if he'd ever truly possessed it. A kind of charm he rarely bothered to feign anymore. It worked. She keyed in her code and then held the door open for him, her smile wide and inviting.

He wasn't looking for that kind of invitation.

He went into a different elevator than she'd chosen and waited for it to carry him to the top floor. He felt out of place here, and yet, being away from the palace brought its own relief.

His jaw tightened as the lift rose, tension bunching his muscles to the point of pain by the time the doors slid open. The hallway was narrow, the building broadcasting its age with each creak of the floorboards. Dampness hung in the air, clung to his clothes, his skin, another side effect of the unpleasant climate.

It reminded him of a jail cell. He had never had a reason to come to the United States before. His place was in Attar, in the broad expanse of the desert. Though, now that his duties kept him close to the palace, it felt nearly as foreign as this cold, damp place.

Since his plane had touched down, he'd been struck by the constant wetness. A chill that soaked through everything, wrapped itself around his bones.

Or maybe the chill wasn't something that could be

blamed on the weather. If he were honest, he would admit that he'd been cold for more than six weeks now. Ever since the word had come about the death of his brother and sister-in-law.

And now there was this.

The child. He made it a goal of his to avoid children, babies in particular. But there would be no avoiding this.

He paused at the door that had a thirteen bolted to it and knocked. He could not remember the last time he'd knocked.

"Just a second." There was a crashing noise, a loud curse and the wail of a baby, then footsteps. He could hear someone leaning against the door. Checking the peephole most likely.

In which case he doubted he would be given admittance. Something else he could not remember facing at any time in his recent memory, at least outside of a combat situation.

He heard a shuffling noise and imagined that the woman who was behind the door was now leaning against it, not opening it, as she'd just seen who was on the other side.

But there was no benefit to Chloe James hiding from him. None at all.

"Chloe James?" he said.

"What?" Her response was muffled by the heavy door between them.

"I am Sheikh Sayid al Kadar, regent of Attar."

"Regent, you say? Interesting. Attar. Nice country I hear. In northern Africa right near—"

"I am aware of the geography of my country, as are you, in ways that go beyond textbook knowledge. You and I both know this."

"Do we?"

There was a sharp spike in the crying, the volume rising, the tone growing more shrill. Loud in the contained environment. Louder behind the apartment door, he imagined.

"Um, I'm busy," Chloe said. "You've woken up the baby now and I have to get him back to sleep so..."

"That is what I'm here about, Chloe. The baby."

"He's cranky right now. But I'll see if I can fit you into his diary."

"Ms. James," he said, aiming for civility. He could push the door in with relative ease, but he doubted that was the right way to go for this. He didn't usually care. But not causing an international incident was a high priority to him at the moment, and he imagined breaking in and simply taking the child might create one. "If you will let me in we can discuss the circumstances of the situation we find ourselves in."

"What situation?"

"The baby."

"What do you want with him?"

"Exactly what my brother wanted with him. A legal agreement has been signed, and you should know exactly what it says, as yours was one of the signatures. I have it in my possession. Either I go through the court system, or we discuss it now."

He didn't want to involve the courts of either the United States or Attar. He wanted this to go smoothly, silently, to not make a ripple until he and his advisers were able to devise a story about how the child had survived, and why the child had been kept from the public in the weeks since the sheikh had died.

Before he did any of that, he had to find out just what the situation was. If the papers that had been drawn up were reflective of the truth, or if there had been more to his brother's relationship with Chloe James than was documented anywhere.

That could complicate things. Could prevent him from taking the child with him. And that was not acceptable.

The door opened a crack, a chain keeping it from swinging open all the way, and one wide blue eye, fringed with long dark lashes, peered at him through the opening. "ID?"

He released a frustrated sigh and reached into the inside of his coat, pulling out his wallet and producing his passport, showing it to the eye that was staring at him with distrust. "Satisfied?"

"Not in the least." The door shut and he heard the jingle of the chain, then it opened. "Come in."

He stepped into the room, the cramped feeling of it squeezing down on him. Bookshelves lined the walls, pushing them in, heightening the feeling of tightness. There was a laptop on the coffee table, more books in a stack to the right of it and a white-board on a stand in the corner with another stack of books placed next to it. There was a logic to the placement of everything, and yet the lack of space gave it all a feeling of barely organized chaos. Nothing like the military precision with which he ordered his life.

He let his eyes fall to Chloe next. She was small, her hair a deep, unusual shade of red, her skin pale and freckled. Her breasts were generous, her waist a bit thick. She looked very much like a woman who had just given birth and who had spent the weeks since in a state of sleep deprivation.

She shifted and her hair caught the light, a shock of red-gold burning bright beneath the lamp. If the child was hers genetically, there would be some sign, of that he was certain. She was very unlike his olive-skinned brother and his beautiful, dark-haired bride.

"You realize that you have no security to speak of here," he said. The crying had ceased, everything in the tiny apartment calm now. "If I had wanted to force my way in, I could have done so. And anyone seeking to harm the child could have done so, as well. You do him no favors by keeping him here."

"I didn't have anywhere else to take him," she said.

"And where is the child now?"

"Aden?" she responded, a chill in her tone. "You don't need to see him now, do you?"

"I would like to," he said.

"Why?" She edged around the front of the sofa, as if she meant to block his way. Laughable. She was so petite, and he was a highly trained soldier who could remove a man twice his size without feeling any sort of exertion. He could break her easily if he had a mind to, and she just stood there, a small, flame-haired tigress.

"He is my nephew. My blood," he said.

"I…I didn't think you would feel any connection to him."

"Why not?" It was true that his was not a heart connection, not the sort of family connection she might mean. His was a blood bond, a sworn oath to protect the ruler of his country with his very life if it came to it. It was a connection that he felt in his veins, one he couldn't change or deny. Only death could break it. And in that scenario, the death had better be his own.

She blinked rapidly. "You've never been…close to the family. I mean, Rashid said…"

"Ah. Rashid." Her use of his brother's first name was telling. And not in a good way. In a way that might complicate things. If she was the mother of the child, the biological mother, it would be much more difficult to use the legal documents against her. Difficult, though, not impossible.

And failing that, he would simply create an international incident and bring the child back with him. By force if necessary.

"Yes, Rashid. Why did you say it like that?"

"I'm trying to ascertain the nature of your relationship with my brother."

She crossed her arms beneath her breasts. "Well, I gave birth to his child."

A cold, calm sort of fury washed through him, the ice in his veins chilling the rage as it ran through him. If his brother had done anything to compromise the future of the country…

But his brother was dead. There would be no consequence for Rashid, no matter the circumstances. He was finished now, with this life. And Sayid was left to ensure that Attar did not crumble. That life went on, as smoothly as possible, for the millions of people who called the desert nation home.

"And you drew up this agreement—" he produced a folded stack of papers from the inside of his coat "—so that if anyone caught on to the fact that it wasn't Tamara who gave birth to Aden, they would believe it had been a part of the plan from the beginning?"

"Wait…what?" She curled her lip, one rounded hip cocked to the side.

"You conspired to invent the story about the surrogacy to cover up the relationship that you had with…"

She held both hands up, palms out. "Hey! No. Oh…no. I gave birth to his child, as a surrogate. His and…Tamara's." There was a slight wobble in her voice now and she looked down.

"Why didn't you come to me?" He wasn't certain he believed her answer, but he wasn't going to press, either. Not now.

"I don't…I don't know. I was scared. They were on their way…here when it happened. On their way to the hospital from the airport. I was already in labor, I went a little earlier than anticipated. They were going to have me moved to a private facility, and their doctor was with them during the…everyone who knew was with them."

He looked around the room, his top lip curling. "So you brought him here, to your very insecure apartment, to protect him?"

"No one knew I was here."

"It took my men less than twenty-four hours from the discovery of your existence to pinpoint your location, and for me to come to your front door. You are lucky that I am the one who found you. Lucky that it wasn't an enemy of my brother, of Attar."

"I couldn't be sure that you wouldn't be an enemy to Aden."

"Be sure of that now."

Chloe raised her gaze and met hard, dark eyes. She couldn't believe that Sayid al Kadar was in her living room. She'd been watching the news about Attar carefully since Aden's birth. Had seen the man assume power with ease and grace, an almost eerie calm, amidst a tragedy that had rocked a nation.

The sheikh and his wife were dead. As was their unborn heir.

So everyone had assumed.

But what no one knew was that the sheikh and sheikha had used a surrogate. And that the surrogate, and the child, were safe.

She'd had no idea what to do. When the royals' private doctor hadn't materialized during delivery, and then Tamara and Rashid hadn't come, either...

She could still feel it, the sick, cold dread that had washed over her. She'd known. She'd just known. And then she'd asked a nurse to turn the television on and it had been everywhere, on every channel. The loss of Attar's royal family and the doctor to the royal family, killed in an accident on a highway in the Pacific Northwest.

And all she'd been able to do was hold the baby— the baby that wasn't hers, the baby that was never supposed to be hers, the baby who had no one but her—close to her chest and try not to dissolve completely.

In the weeks since she'd been in a daze. Mourning her half sister, Tamara, though she'd barely known her, and trying to decide what she was supposed to do with Aden. Trying to decide if she should trust his uncle. Because if it was revealed that Aden was alive, then Sayid was not the ruler of Attar, he was merely regent.

And the idea of what he might do to preserve his position had frightened her. She knew it was unlikely, ridiculous, even. Rashid had never spoken badly of his younger brother, and neither had Tamara.

Still, this sort of strange, never-before-felt protectiveness had her in its grip, digging into her like claws, not releasing its hold. Aden was her nephew, and because of that, she did have a connection to him, but it was more. She'd imagined that it wouldn't be. She didn't want children, after all. Had never seen herself as the maternal type.

But she'd carried him in her body. Nurtured him in that way. No matter what she'd believed, it wasn't a bond that she could simply break. Her head knew one thing, but her body firmly believed another.

"And you didn't think to contact the palace?" Sayid asked, his voice deep. Hard.

"Rashid asked that it be kept confidential. I signed legal documents saying that I would never divulge my involvement. If they had wanted to include you, they would have."

"So all of this was out of loyalty?"

"Well…yes."

"And how much were you paid?" he asked.

Her cheeks heated. "Enough." She had accepted payment, and she was hardly going to apologize. Surrogates were paid for the service, and while she'd done it in part because Tamara was her half sister, she'd also done it out of a need for the money. Even with all of her scholarships, graduate school was costly. And independence was an absolute necessity for her, which meant money held a lot of importance in her world.

"Loyalty. I see."

"Of course I was paid," she said. "I wanted to do this for them, but honestly, carrying a child and giving birth? It's a very big deal, as I have spent the past ten or so months now discovering. I won't feel guilty for taking what I was offered."

"And why exactly did you *want* to do this for him?" He was still looking at her with a dark, angry light in his eyes and she had a feeling he still didn't really believe that she'd had no involvement with Rashid.

"Because of Tamara. She's my half sister. And I'm not surprised you didn't know. We didn't meet until a couple of years ago, and we've never had the chance to become close." Finding out she'd had a half sister had been such an extraordinary moment. Tamara had found her, using the new resources available to her as the sheikh's wife.

Chloe had been in awe of her when they first met. The sheikha, her sister. But it wasn't her beauty or power that had captivated Chloe, it was the fact that she had a new chance at family. Something whole, tangible and shining where before there had been nothing but broken pieces, pain and regret.

They hadn't had the chance to spend a lot of time together. They lived a half a world away from each other, and meetings had been sporadic, but wonderful. A friendship that had been bursting with the possibility to be a bond she'd never had the chance to have before. And now she never would. That new, beautiful thing was shattered, too. There would never be any family for her, not ever.

Except Aden.

Her heart ached just thinking about the tiny baby sleeping in the bassinet in her room. She didn't know what she felt for him. Didn't know what to do with him. Didn't know how she was supposed to give him up. Or keep him. She couldn't imagine doing either, which put her right where she was now.

Studying for midterms with a baby that wouldn't let her sleep, living in fear of the moment she was currently standing in. For one brief, dark second she hated her life.

A year ago she'd been starting grad school, on her way to getting her doctorate in theoretical physics, and now she was living in an existence that didn't seem like it could possibly be hers.

Grieving the sister she'd barely known, the possibility of something that had never gotten to be, struggling to finish her coursework. Raising a baby.

And in that same, ugly moment, she imagined handing Aden to his uncle and telling him to take good care of him.

When she'd agreed to all of this, clearly, she'd never imagined that keeping Aden would even be a possibility, and now she felt as if she was in a hellish limbo, having tiny tastes of what could be, what might have been. If she'd been different. If her life had been different.

If could never really be her life. Not really.

She took a deep breath, fighting the wave of exhaustion that grabbed her by the throat and started shaking her hard.

Sayid's face remained impassive, his eyes the only tell, showing a hint of hard, bitter regret. "I am sorry for your loss."

"And I'm sorry for yours."

"Not just mine," he said. "My country's. My people's. Aden is their future ruler. The hope of the future."

"He's a baby," she said, her voice hollow in her ears. Aden was so tiny, so helpless. Robbed of his mother, his real mother. The one who was prepared for him, who was ready to give everything to raise him. The one who was capable of it.

All he'd had for the first six weeks of his life was her. She'd never held a baby before he was born, and now she was fumbling her way through caring for one round the clock. She was exhausted. She wanted to cry all the time. She did cry sometimes.

"Yes," Sayid said, "he is a baby. One who was born into something much bigger than he is. But then, you and I both know that was the purpose behind his birth."

"Partly. Rashid and Tamara wanted him very much." That much had been clear, the desire for a child pouring from Tamara's every word when she'd made her impassioned request.

"I'm certain they did, but the only reason a blood bond was so important, the only reason adoption could not be considered, was the need for an heir that was part of the al Kadar line."

She knew that. That day seemed like an eternity ago. Tamara had come for a visit, but this time, her dark eyes weren't glittering with laughter, but tears. Tears as she told Chloe of her most recent miscarriage. Of how she kept losing her babies. Of the depth of her desire for a child of her own, of her need to give birth for the kingdom.

And then she'd made her request. So big. So altering.

You'll be compensated, and of course, once the child is born he'll return to Attar with us. But you'll be a part of bringing your nephew into the world. More family. For both of us.

And Chloe ached for family. For a web of support like she'd never had before.

And so she'd convinced herself that being pregnant for nine months really wouldn't be a hardship. And that at the end of it, Tamara and Rashid would have everything they needed and that Chloe would have helped bring a new life into the world. And that a whole lot of her financial problems would be solved.

It had seemed an easy thing to do. A small thing for the only family who seemed to care about her at all. Simple.

Of course, once the morning sickness had hit the "easy" thing had seemed a long-ago, laughable thought. Then there had been the weight gain, the sore breasts, the stretch marks. And of course, labor and delivery.

Nothing about it had been easy.

But in the peaceful quiet just after giving birth, that brief surreal moment in time, before she'd found out about Tamara and Rashid's deaths, as she'd looked down at the tiny, screaming baby in her arms, all of the fragmented pieces in her life had seemed to unite, to create a clear and beautiful picture. As if she'd done what she was here to do. As if Aden was her finest, most important achievement. Now or ever.

That was before the world had broken apart again, before things had been smashed, destroyed so utterly and completely that she had no idea how it would ever be fixed again.

She'd been a zombie for six weeks. Caring for Aden, caring for herself when she could, studying, sort of. Slipping beneath the surface, certain that she was going to drown.

Sayid's appearance was both a salvation and damnation rolled into one.

"I know. But right now he…. What do you want to do with him?"

"I intend to do what was always meant to be done. To take him back to his home. To his people. His palace. It is his right, and it is my duty to protect those rights."

"And who will raise him?"

"Tamara had hired the best nannies already, the very best caregivers in the world. After I announce that he is…alive, everything will go as it was meant to." There was a strange sort of calm to his voice, one that made her wonder what was going on beneath the surface.

"When did you find out?" she asked.

"Yesterday. I was going through my brother's safe, his most private documents, and I found the surrogacy agreement. For the first time in six weeks… some hope."

"You really did find us quickly."

"I have sources. More than that, you aren't very well hidden."

"I was afraid," she said, her voice a choked whisper.

"Of what?" he asked.

"Everything." That was the honest truth. Her life had been marked by gut-churning anxiety and fear since Tamara's death. Every day felt temporary, and like an eternity. "I was afraid you wouldn't want the competition. That you wouldn't want to lose your new position."

Sayid's dark eyes hardened, his lips thinning. "I was not raised to rule, Chloe James, I was raised to fight. In my country, that is the function of the second born son. I am a warrior. The High Sheikh must have compassion and strength. Fairness. I was not trained to have those things. I was trained to carry out orders, to be merciless in my pursuit of preserving my people and my country. Which I will do now, at any cost. This is not about what I want, it is about what is best."

She believed him. The evidence of the truth was there in his voice, in the flat, emotionlessness. He was a soldier, a machine created to carry out orders with swift, efficient execution.

And he wanted to take Aden with him.

She blinked, feeling dizzy. "So, essentially, you're the ax man of the al Kadar family?" It just slipped out. She wasn't prone to speaking without thinking. Thinking was her stock-in-trade. But she felt off balance now, not sure what to say or do. There was no textbook for this situation, no amount of studying that could have prepared her for it. No amount of reasoning.

"My path was set from my first breath."

"And so is Aden's," she said, her lips numb, cold shock spreading through her. She'd always known that the little boy sleeping in the bassinet in her bedroom was meant for greatness, greatness that had nothing to do with her. But these past weeks…they had been out of time. Something so different from anything else she'd experienced. Miserable, and beautiful. Temporary. And in them, it had been easy, necessary even, to ignore the reality of his destiny.

"He needs to come back home. Your life can go back to the way it was. To the way you planned for it to be."

She could finished school, get her doctorate. Take a teaching position at a university, or maybe get a job at a research institute. A girl and her whiteboard. It would be a beautiful and simple existence. One where she spent her time analyzing mysteries of the universe that had a hope of actually being solved, something that seemed impossible in interpersonal relationships. Which was one reason she rarely bothered with those, not beyond casual friendships at least.

That was the future that Sayid was offering right now. The chance to go back to the way things were. Like nothing had changed.

She looked down, saw the rounded bump where once her stomach had been flat. And she thought of the child, sleeping in the next room, the child who had grown inside of her body, the child she'd given birth to, and she knew that everything had changed. Everything.

There was no going back.

"I can't just let you take him."

"You were going to let Rashid and Tamara take him."

"They were his parents, and they were…meant to be with him."

"His place in Attar goes deeper than that," he said, his voice uncompromising.

"He'll be confused, I…I'm the only mother he knows." She'd never put voice to that thought until now. But she'd been caring for him. Breastfeeding him. She'd given birth to him, and even though, genetically, he was not her son, he was something, something that was essential in some ways.

"You do not wish to go back to your old life? To get back to how it was?"

In some ways she did. Badly. Just thinking about it, about what she'd have to give up, to either have Aden or to have things the way they were, made her feel as if she was being torn in two.

"I don't think it can," she said, the truth, another thing she'd left unacknowledged for as long as possible. "It's not the same. It never will be again." A fact, irrefutable as far as she was concerned, no mathematical equations required to prove it.

"Then what do you propose?" he asked, muscular arms crossed over his broad chest.

Just then, Aden stirred, his sharp cry loud in the silence of the apartment. That single, shrill cry, pierced her heart, made her ache everywhere.

"Take me to Attar."

CHAPTER TWO

"ABSOLUTELY NOT," SAYID said, striding from the living room and heading toward the bedroom, where Aden was crying plaintively.

"Where the hell do you think you're going?" Something inside of her snapped, watching that large, predatory body walking toward the baby's room.

He stopped, turning to face her. "I am going to collect my nephew, as is my right." He held the papers out, the surrogacy agreement, which she had signed, knowing full well what it meant. Papers she'd signed without regret. Papers that said Aden belonged to the royal family, to Attar, and not to her. Never to her.

He turned away again and her feet carried her, without her volition, quickly, to where he was going. She put her hands on his shoulders and tugged him backward. His shoulders were thick and muscled, his frame solid and immovable beneath her hands. The kind of man she normally feared.

For a blinding second, she had a flash of what

it would be like if he swept the back of his hand across her face. She knew just how that looked. Hard packed muscle coming up against a petite frame. Knew what it looked like to see a woman crumbled on the ground, broken and bleeding, the victim of masculine power.

Sayid didn't do that. He stopped, not because she'd had any effect on him. He could have shrugged her off of him with ease, but he didn't. Instead, he turned back to her slowly, his eyes dark, filled with heat and fury. "What are you doing?" he asked.

"You're not just going to go in there and scoop him up and carry him off to the desert," she said, her pulse pounding in her throat. "You might be the sheikh in your country but here you're just an intruder in my house and if I have to mace your ass and then call the cops I will do it." Anger drove her, a rage that made her shake, made her body quiver down to her bones. It banished her fear, fear of retribution, of violence at his hands.

Because right now, Aden was the weakest one here. And if she didn't stand for him then no one would.

"Interesting," he said, his voice coated in ice, "your file said you were a scientist, I expected more reserve."

"And you're supposed to be a leader, I expected you to have a little more of a deft hand at negotiation." For some reason, he reacted to that. A small reaction, a small flare of something much deeper and more frightening than the anger from before. But it didn't stop her. "Did you honestly think I would let you walk in and take my baby?"

Sayid straightened, his eyes black, blank again, absent of malice, or anything else. "He is not your baby."

The truth hit, cold and hard, at the same time as the realization of what she'd said. "I know that. But I've been caring for him. I breastfeed him," she said, desperation building in her chest, "you can't just come in and take him."

"You were meant to surrender him, and you know it to be true."

"To Tamara," she said, her voice rough. "I was meant to hand him to his mother, my sister, but she wasn't there. His mother is dead. And no one knew about him. I didn't know what to do, who to tell. The only other person who's ever held him have been medical personnel, and you want to...to take him away."

"I don't want to take him from you," he said, his jaw tight, his tone hard. "I must do what is best for Attar. I am not here to disrupt your little game of house. But Aden is not your son, and he does not belong here."

"Then let me go there."

"And reveal the secret that Rashid was so desperate to protect?"

She shook her head. "No. No...I could be...the nanny."

"For the next sixteen years? Until he comes of age?"

She didn't have the next sixteen years to spend in Attar. She had a life here. She had friends. And school. A student teacher position starting in the fall. All she had to do was wean herself away. There was no other choice, no other choice beyond making a clean break now, and that she knew she couldn't do.

She shook her head. "No...not that I..." She swallowed and looked down. "But maybe...if he could be here with me for a few months even. Six months." She didn't know why she'd said six months. Only that it was time. More time to try and wrap her head around everything that had happened to her. More time to hold on to Aden when she really should just let go.

She started to walk into the room, toward Aden, and Sayid caught her arm, dark eyes blazing into hers. "Tell me this," he said, his tone hard, "and be honest. You were only the surrogate, right? There was nothing between you and my brother?"

"Nothing," she said.

"I need to know. Because there can be no surprises. No scandal."

"Rashid loved Tamara. He would never..."

Sayid nodded. "He did. It's true. But I have seen the things men can do, thoughtless things that cause a world of pain, and I would not put it past him. Not even him. Everyone is capable of evil."

Evil, she had seen. In the most seemingly innocuous of men. His hard hold on her, fingers biting into her skin, was a reminder of that. "Even you?"

"Everyone is capable of evil," he repeated.

"Well, your brother did no such evil. Not with me." The idea was completely laughable. Or it would have been if Sayid hadn't been so serious. "I did this because of Tamara. Because she was my family. And now Aden is my family."

He released his hold on her. "Good. I cannot afford any complications."

Anger spiked in her again, a welcome reprieve from the hopelessness that was starting to overwhelm her. "Well, I couldn't afford any complications, either, Your Royal Sheikhiness. Yet I seem to have nothing but complications at the moment."

"I could make them go away," he said, his voice cold, uncompromising. "Can make it so your life goes back to the way it was before."

"Could you take the pain with you?" she said, desperation tearing at her as she realized, fully, just how impossible a situation she was in. "Can you make it so it's like it never happened? Make me forget that I carried a child and gave birth to him? That I cared for him for the first six weeks of his life? Can you make him forget?"

"He will be given everything in Attar. No comfort will be denied him. This is not a decision to make with your emotions. This is a decision that you must think about logically."

Logic had long been a comfort to her. Fact, reason, had carried her through a childhood filled with chaos. But logic couldn't win here. For the first time, her heart was louder than her head. "Will you love him?" she asked.

His black eyes were cold. "I would die for him."

"It's not the same thing."

"But it is the promise I can make." Men, men and their promises, had been something she'd spent a lifetime avoiding. She'd watched men break their promises, again and again, and as an adult she'd chosen to never put stock in them. But this promise, this vow, that seemed to come from deep inside of him, from his soul, was something she couldn't doubt. She felt it echoing inside of her, down on a subatomic level. "He is my king. The heir to the throne of Attar. He has my allegiance, both as my future leader and as a member of my family."

"He's a baby," she said, the word catching in her throat. "Right now, that's the important thing."

"He is a child," Sayid said, "I know that. But he will never be like other children. He is meant to rule, it is a part of who he is. Who he was born to be. We all have a burden to bear in this life," he continued, his voice softer now. "We all have a purpose that must be met. This is his."

"But…but," she stuttered, desperation digging its claws into her. She took a breath and redirected, scrolling through her mind for information she could use. Knowledge was power, now and always. "I understand that he's the heir, but fundamentally, he's a baby. Taking him from me, from his caregiver, now could cause damage, especially as I assume there will be staff caring for him?"

Sayid shrugged broad shoulders. "Of course." Because Sayid would not be involved, not on a personal level. He might be willing to lay down his life for his nephew, but changing diapers was another thing altogether.

"I grant you, child development, and biology in general, are not my areas of expertise, but I know they've done studies on these early life experiences and they're crucial to the emotional well-being of a person. If they aren't given the proper attention now, they may never be able to form attachments in the future."

Sayid regarded her, his eyes dark, fathomless. "That I believe."

"I mean, they've actually looked at CAT scans of the brains of children who have experienced stable nurturing and those who haven't. It changes them on a physical level. Parts of their brain cease to function properly and…and…I doubt you want that for a ruler, do you?"

"Naturally not," he said, clipped.

"I've been…I've been taking care of him," she said, her throat tightening. "Breastfeeding him. What do you think it would do to him to be separated from me? I'm his only stability."

"And what do you think letting him cry is doing to his psyche?" he asked, his tone hard.

She brushed past him and went toward the bassinet, her heart in her throat. She bent down and pulled him gently into her arms. Holding him still didn't feel natural. It made her nervous. Always afraid she wasn't supporting his head just right. And the soft spot. Yes, she knew there was a reason for it to be there, but it terrified her to the core. It highlighted just how vulnerable he was. How breakable.

Sayid watched Chloe pull the child in to her body, her arms wrapped around him securely but gently. She didn't look like a natural, didn't look at ease. Her blue eyes were huge, her lips tightened into a firm line, denoting her fear and concentration.

The sight created a strange tightness in his chest, a heaviness that made it difficult to breathe. Her discomfort was evident. The fact that she didn't want to do this, or that she, at the very least, didn't love it, was evident. Yet she felt compelled to fight to stay in Aden's life. Had cared for him, protected him, from the moment he was born. Because she was bonded to him, her loyalty deep and strong.

Loyalty he understood. Honor. The need to protect others at the expense of yourself. He saw it all in that moment, etched across her face.

"Six months," he said.

She looked up at him, her expression cautious. "Six months of what?"

"You may come back to Attar, to the palace, for six months and serve as his nanny for the purposes of maintaining the fiction of his birth for the public eye. It's a reasonable step. Logical to believe we secured a woman who is able to nurse the child, as he's lost his mother."

"I...oh...I..."

"I will make the announcement to the press that Aden was born just before Tamara's death and that until we knew his health was stable we wanted no intrusion."

"What will people think...that you kept something like that from them?"

"They will understand," he said, his voice, his certainty, echoing in the room. "There is no other option. Rashid wished to keep it a secret, and so it will be kept secret."

"Tamara said...she said if people knew they might think that it was down to some sort of faithlessness on her part."

He shook his head once. "Not everyone. Anyone who knew her would never have thought so. But certainly yes, you have factions of the population who regard infertility as a link to some sort of sin on the woman's part."

"They wanted to avoid that," she said. "And now... now it's even more important, isn't it? Now that he's the only one left."

She looked down at the top of Aden's fuzzy head, her expression dazed.

"Yes," he said. The helplessness of the child, his tiny size, delicate body, filled him with a sense of unease. He had the sense of fingers being curled around his neck, cutting off his air. He had felt ill at ease ever since assuming the throne. He was not a diplomat, not a man to sit and do paperwork or make polite conversation with visiting dignitaries.

The press knew it. Took every chance to compare him with the sheikh they had lost. The sheikh that had been born to rule with the one that had only been bred to fight.

And now there was this. This baby. This woman. The child might very well be his salvation, the one that would take his place on the throne. But right now...now he was a baby. Small. Helpless.

It made him think of another helpless life, one he had been powerless to save. And it added another brick to the weight of responsibility on his shoulders. He shook the feeling off. Emotion, regret, the pain of the past, had no place in his life, not even in such a small capacity.

He had learned that lesson early, and he had learned it well. When a man felt much, he could lose much. And so he had been shaped into a man who had nothing left to lose. A man who could act decisively, quickly. He couldn't worry about his own safety. Could worry about being good. He had to find lighter shades of gray in the darkness. Do what was the most right, and the least wrong. Without regret.

Looking at Aden, his nephew, the last piece of his brother's legacy, tested him. But he could not afford to break now, couldn't afford a crack in his defenses. So he crushed it tight inside of him, buried it deep, beneath the rock and stone walls he had built up around his heart.

"Six months?" she asked, raising blue eyes to meet his.

"Six months. And after that you will carry on as you intended to. That is what you want ultimately, isn't it?"

She nodded slowly, her fingers drifting idly over Aden's back. "Yes. That's what I want."

"And that's what you will have. Now pack your things, we need to leave."

"But…I have midterms…I…"

"I can call your professors and arrange to have you take the tests remotely."

"I don't know if they'll let me."

That made him laugh. "They will not tell me no."

"You don't have to fight my battles for me," she said.

"I fight everyone's battles for them," he said. "It's who I am. As you will soon discover."

Sayid's parting words rang in her ears as she packed, her fingers numb while she folded her clothes and stuffed them into her suitcase. She still felt that same numbness as she boarded the private plane that was sitting on the tarmac at Portland International Airport. It had spread to her face, her lips. And she felt cold.

Shock, maybe. Or, judging by the sharp stab of pain that assaulted her when the door to the plush, private airplane closed, maybe the shock from the past six weeks was finally wearing off. She wanted it back. Wanted to be wrapped up in the fuzzy cocoon she'd been living in, where she hadn't been able to see more than an hour ahead. One foot in front of the other, just trying to survive. Trying to look at the future as a whole was too demanding.

Six months.

She held Aden a little bit closer and leaned back in the plush, roomy seat, examining the cabin of the plane. It wasn't like anything she'd ever seen before. Being in Attar would feel like being in another world, and she'd expected that. She hadn't expected everything to feel so different the moment she stepped into Sayid's domain, even on American soil.

Sayid sat across from the seat she sat in with Aden. His arms were resting on the back of the couch, his body in a pose that she imagined was meant to mimic relaxation. She wasn't fooled, even for a moment. Sayid wasn't a man who relaxed easily, if ever. His eyes were sharp, his body clearly on alert.

He looked as though he could spring into deadly, efficient action at any moment. Like a panther preparing for a strike.

"Handy that you had a passport ready, expediting Aden's was much easier than having to do it for the both of you. Have you done a lot of traveling?" he asked.

She knew these weren't idle questions. He still

didn't trust her, not really. Which was fine since she certainly didn't trust him.

"I went to see the Large Hadron Collider in Switzerland a couple of years ago. It was a brilliant opportunity."

The left side of his mouth lifted upward in a poor imitation of a smile. "Most women I've known would consider a sale on a designer handbag a brilliant opportunity."

She could tell he was trying to make her angry. She wasn't sure why he was trying to make her angry, only that he was. "I like a good handbag as much as the next woman. But if you really want to watch my eyes light up talk string theory to me."

"I am afraid I would be outmatched," he said, inclining his head. She'd earned some respect with that response.

He was testing her. Jackass. Nothing she wasn't used to. Men didn't like being shown up by women. The men in her academic circle were threatened by her mind, by her successes. So they were always looking for a weakness. Good thing she didn't have one. Not when it came to her mind, at least.

"You ought to be," she said. "But if you wanted to talk…I don't know, Arabian stallions I might be outmatched."

He laughed. "You think my expertise lies in stallions?"

"A guess. A stereotypical guess, I confess."

He shrugged. "I'm not one for horses myself. Military vehicles are more my domain. Weapons. Artillery. How to stage an ambush in the dunes. Things like that."

The statement maybe should have shocked her, but it didn't. There was nothing that seemed remotely safe about Sayid al Kadar. He exuded danger, darkness. She wasn't one to cultivate a lot of interpersonal relationships, but danger was one thing she'd learned to see early on. A matter of survival.

"Well, I can't make much conversation about that."

"Silence would be your solution, then?" he asked, arching one dark brow.

"I wouldn't say no to it. It's been a long twenty-four hours." It had taken some time to get the documentation to allow Aden to fly.

"The press will be gathering in Attar as we speak. Jockeying for position in front of the palace."

"Do they know what you're announcing?"

He shook his head. "No. I will announce it after the results of the DNA test are back. A precaution, you understand. The testing must be done to prevent rumors of us bringing in a child who is not truly an al Kadar."

"This royalty business is complicated," she said.

"It's not. Not really. Everyone has a role, and as long as they are there to fill it, everything keeps moving." There was a bleakness wrapped around those words, a resignation that made her curious.

The plane's engines roared to life and she curled

herself around Aden, holding him securely as they started down the runway.

"He makes you nervous," Sayid said.

She looked up, knowing exactly what he meant. "I don't have any experience with babies."

"And you haven't been waiting around dying to have your own."

"I'm twenty-three. I don't exactly feel ready for it. But...even in the future I didn't have plans of... marriage and motherhood." Quite the opposite, she'd always intended to avoid both like the plague. Had done so quite neatly for her entire life.

"Yet you protect him. Like a tigress with her cub." Everything was a casual observation from him, no heat of conviction. No emotion at all.

"There are survival instincts that are born into us," she said, looking down at Aden's head, his hair fuzzy and wild, standing on end. "An innate need to propagate the species and ensure its survival."

"Is that all?" he asked.

She shook her head, her throat tightening. "No."

"It is good. Good that he has an aunt who loves him."

Yes. It was completely natural for her to love him. To feel like he was a piece of her. He was, after all. Her nephew. Her only remaining family.

The only remaining family that she acknowledged. Her parents were no longer a part of her life. She never intended on speaking to them, going back and peering into the ugliness that was their marriage. She'd escaped it, and she never intended on going back.

Aden represented her last link with family. Her last chance. It was no wonder the bond was so strong. And he had no one. At least, he'd had no one. It had been just the two of them, holed up in the apartment, surviving.

"I do love him," she said.

"It pleases me." She noticed he didn't return the sentiment, and that none of the pleasure he spoke of was reflected in his tone. She searched his face, looked into those hard, black eyes to see if she could find some hidden depth of emotion. Some tenderness for the tiny baby in her arms.

There was nothing there.

Nothing but an endless sea of darkness, a black hole, that seemed to pull light in, only to extinguish it.

"I went to live with my uncle, Kalid, when I was seven. I don't know if Rashid ever mentioned that," he said.

"No." She'd barely ever spoken to her brother-in-law. He wasn't usually present during her visits with Tamara.

"It is common, with the warrior children, to go and learn from the one currently holding the position."

"So young?"

"It is necessary," he said. "As you mentioned, early childhood experiences play strongly into how you will be as an adult. Something so important could not be left to chance."

"What…what do you mean?"

"Because to be a perfect soldier, you can't be a perfect man," he said. "You have to be broken first, so that it can't happen later. At the hands of your enemies."

His tone was perfectly smooth, perfectly conversational. Betraying nothing of the underlying horror. But it was there. In his eyes.

It was easy to imagine getting pulled into that darkness. Easy to imagine getting lost in it. In him. The feeling that created rocked her deeply, gripped her stomach and squeezed tight.

She'd never had a thought like that before, had never felt, even for a moment, the sudden, violent pull to someone like she felt for Sayid.

She turned away, redirecting her focus. This six months was for Aden. A chance to introduce him to his home. To give him the transition they both needed.

It was not a time for her to get drawn in by a man with dark eyes and an even darker soul.

CHAPTER THREE

IF THE PLANE WAS LIKE another world, the Attari palace was something beyond that. On the outskirts of a city that was a collision between the old world and the new, was the seat of the royal family's power. Gleaming stone, jade, jasper and obsidian, inlaid in intricate patterns over the walls and floors, the edges gilded, catching fire in the dry, harsh sun that painted the air with waves of heat.

The only green was in the palace gardens, the lush plants an extravagant example of wealth. A surplus of water in a dry place. The fountains spoke of the same excess, statues carved of young women, endlessly pouring water into the pools below.

The palace itself was shielded from the heat, the thick stone walls providing cover and insulation.

Her entire apartment could fit in the entryway of the palace, pillars wrapped in gold supporting ceilings inlaid with precious stones.

For the fist time, Chloe was ashamed that she'd asked her sister into her apartment. Tamara had never said anything about the shabby little one bedroom, but…but this was what her sister had been accustomed to. And Chloe hadn't had a clue. She'd known her sister had lived in a palace, but her mind, so dedicated to number and fact, could never have imagined it was this grand.

The suite of rooms they were installed in had been set up for Aden and the nanny. Her room was expansive, a high ceiling with a star pattern arching over the opulent bed, white pillars, carved with scenes of camels wandering the desert, stationed throughout as support.

Chloe wandered in, placing her hand over one of the camels. Amber, she realized, set into a golden background, representing the Attari sand. One pillar would easily pay for a year of her college tuition, a sobering realization indeed.

She followed the flow of the room into Aden's, which was connected to hers. The bed that had been prepared for him the focal point of the room. Blue with swaths of fabric draped from the ceiling that covered the little crib, making it look like a throne fit for a very tiny prince.

Which he was really.

"An improvement, isn't it?" She placed him gently into the bed, her fingertips lingering on his round belly.

The sight of him, so small, in the plush bed made her throat tighten. This room had been prepared by Tamara. Prepared for a son she had never gotten the chance to hold. Hadn't even been able to carry in her womb.

Chloe had done that, and she had hated it. Had been miserable through the whole pregnancy while her sister, who would never even know her child, had longed to carry the baby and hadn't been able to.

Tears stung her eyes. She wanted to rail at the world. At the injustice of it. Nothing made sense in the world. Nothing. There was no reason. And she, she most especially, seemed to have no way of controlling it. She'd tried. She'd planned. And everything had fallen apart.

Anguish threatened to overwhelm her, to wrap bony fingers around her throat and squeeze her tight, cutting off her air.

"Is everything to your liking?"

She turned and saw Sayid standing in the opening to Aden's room, his shoulders military straight, his hands clasped behind his back, his expression hard. In that moment, she envied him. He saw things clearly, in black and white. There was no confusion for him. No anger. No grief. He was simply doing what had to be done, and for him, that seemed to be enough.

Nothing she did felt like enough. Nothing felt right.

Not even this, and it was the only thing she could think to do.

"It's beautiful, but I imagine you know that."

His shoulders broke rank long enough to shrug.

"The palace is done in the traditional Attari style. It is not so unusual here."

"Ah yes, well, I can see how a castle made of semi-precious stones would get tiresome after a while," she said drily.

"I find most anything preferable to an enemy prison, in that regard the palace does nicely. It is nicer to look at than a prison cell at the very least."

"Is that all that makes it better?" she asked, laughing, a nervous shaky sound.

"In some ways," he said slowly, "it is shockingly similar to prison." His statement begged a question but he pressed on too quickly. "Your schooling has been worked out. The classes will be broadcasted onto a website you can log in to. That way you can view the lectures in addition to having your reading material on hand."

"Labs? I mainly work in the realm of the theoretical, which means more mathematics than actual physical experiments, but there is some lab work to be done."

"It will likely have to be deferred, but that's fine, as well. You're a well-liked student."

"Most everyone at this level is. If you're pursuing physics this far, it's a passion."

"And you are…passionate about it?"

The way he said "passionate" made her stomach curl in slightly, and she wasn't sure why. "Yes."

"What about it do you find so fascinating?"

She looked down at Aden. "I like to know why.

The why of everything." She looked back at Sayid. "Though, I've discovered there are things in life that simply aren't explainable. I know about the building blocks of life, but I haven't exactly figured out how to make everything make sense yet."

"Not everything can be explained," he said.

"But it's my great quest to see if it can be."

He shook his head. "I can tell you right now, there is too much in this world that does not make sense and never will. Greed makes men do terrible things, desire for power. The desire for control."

"Survival of the fittest," she said.

"Sure. But I've seen it. I've seen what people are willing to do. It does not make sense, trust me."

She did. His voice rang with a depth of understanding that echoed inside of her. Images of violence flashed behind her eyes.

Sometimes there really was no reason.

"To the best of my ability," she said, trying to shake off the memories, "I try to make sense of it all. To find the absolutes, the things that can't be argued or denied. Theoretically, it should make my life feel more ordered. More in control."

"How is that working out?"

"Like hell, actually."

He nodded slowly. "Yes, that has been my experience, as well. In particular, in regards to recent events."

"Common ground," she said. "Unexpected."

"Perhaps not quite so unexpected," he said. "I see

things in much the same way you do. Black or white. Yes or no."

She looked at Aden, love, pain, filling her. "I used to see things that way. More than I do now."

Sayid looked away from her, his dark eyes scanning the room. The moment of connection was broken. "There will be two other nannies in my employ while you are here. One to work in the night, the other to help handle him while you study."

"And I'm the…wet nurse. Part of the prince's team?"

He looked back at her and for a moment, she thought she saw a teasing light in his eyes. "A prince needs a team. Calling you another nanny would do, though, no need to be dramatic. Or medieval."

She looked back down at Aden and the enormity of what he would face filled her, overwhelmed her. It was unfair, she knew, because even if his parents had lived, his future would be the same. He was, as Sayid had pointed out, born to rule.

But right then it didn't seem fair. Didn't seem fair that the expectations of a nation should rest on the shoulders of this tiny baby.

"Why can't you just do it?" she whispered. "You were going to rule. Can't you take it from him?"

She chanced a glance at him. His eyes were trained on the wall, distance. Dark. "I would do what had to be done, but I am not the man to lead this country."

"But you're doing it until Aden is old enough to—"

"I will do what must be done."

"Nothing more?" she asked, not bothering to keep the bitterness from her tone.

He looked at her then, and she studied the hard lines of his face, the light that filtered through the windows deepening the grooves by his mouth, making the line between his brows appear deeper. It revealed his cares, his pain, the marks, the age, the world had left on him.

"Attar needs hope. A future filled with endless possibilities. With me, they will not get that. Death follows me, Chloe James. I will not bring that on my people, but on their enemies."

He turned and walked back out of the room, and Chloe just watched, tension releasing from her slowly with each step he took away from her, until she was left feeling like wrung-out jelly. She hadn't been conscious of just how tense she'd been until it had started to ease.

She let out a breath and clenched her hands into fists, trying to stop her fingers from shaking. His words echoed in her head, so dark, so certain.

She shook her head, focusing her mind back on Aden. There was too much going on for her to adopt Sayid's issues, as well. And anyway, she imagined he would say he didn't have any. She wandered back into her room, sitting down at the laptop that had already been set up at a corner desk for her. She could at least do some course work, study for her tests. She pushed the on button and waited for it to boot up, scanning the room, the view of the gardens from the double doors.

Today, everything had changed. Again.

"Sheikh Sayid," Sayid's advisor, Malik, walked into the dining room, his eyes fixed on the ground in front of him. It was not the person he'd been expecting. He'd been expecting Chloe, spitting hellfire and brimstone about him taking over her schedule and demanding she have dinner with him. He was not so lucky. "We need to discuss the matter of the press conference that is planned for tomorrow."

"What is there to discuss?" Sayid asked, annoyance coursing through him. He didn't want to talk about the press conference. Didn't want to do anything but eat dinner and treat himself to a punishing workout. Something that would numb him and leave him utterly exhausted. After a day locked inside of an office, trapped behind a desk, he felt it was deserved. Necessary.

It was like prison. Even if it was a more comfortable cell. It was also too opulent, too busy. He longed for the simplicity of a desert tent, or at the very least, the whitewashed walls of the seaside palace he had spent time in as a child.

His aide kept on avoiding his eyes. "You know that the people are…they are restless."

"They do not like me," Sayid said. "That is the crux of the issue."

"You are not…personable."

Sayid laughed, the sound void of humor, his body void of humor. "Am I not?"

"It has been said, Sheikh."

"Not by you, certainly," he said, eyeing the man who had served Rashid so faithfully.

He did meet his eyes this time. "Certainly not."

"It is of no consequence. I am not the permanent ruler of this country. Soon enough, my nephew shall take over and I will go back to my more palatable position outside of the public eye."

"In sixteen years. That is a reality you cannot ignore."

It was the truth. It wasn't like submitting to physical torture. As a ruler he had to lay open pieces of himself, show personality. Be nice. At least when his hands were bound, when he was being whipped, burned, he could shut down the pain, allow it to rest on his skin like armor, recede inside of himself and simply endure. Survive.

But that was not what was required of a ruler. And he knew nothing else.

"Are you questioning my competence?" he asked.

"Not in the least, Sheikh."

"Be sure you do not. You are dismissed."

Malik nodded and turned away from him, walking out the door. Panic, momentary but intense, shivered over Sayid's skin. He would have to face a people who distrusted him tomorrow, would have to find words to speak to them. Words of comfort. Diplomacy.

It simply wasn't what Sayid had been *trained* for.

And trained was precisely the word that should be used. From the time he'd gone into Kalid's care, he'd been conditioned to see life in a certain way.

And at sixteen, it had been cemented. He had been broken, remade. A man who could, physically, endure all.

But he was no diplomat, no compassionate ruler.

All of the civility, the grace and manners, had been bred into Rashid. Sayid had gotten none of it. Sayid was a weapon, a living, breathing weapon. It was all he knew. It was all he'd ever done.

Control was necessary. A drop in control could lead to unspeakable horror. A girl forced into marriage, her child torn from her body against her will. Soldiers captured and killed. Tortured.

His weakness had caused those unspeakable horrors. Cracks in his armor leading others to ruin.

Leading, ruling, would require him to deal with people. Not simply enemies and soldiers. It would require the kind of openness, caring that would create a breach he couldn't afford. One he could already feel deep within his soul. A soul he had not been aware of until recently.

"I don't appreciate you…scheduling my evening without talking to me."

Later than expected, Chloe walked in, her curves encased in a simple black dress. There was nothing particularly sexy about the dress. Nothing modern or interesting in the cut. But the way it flowed over her curves, molded to her breasts, made it spectacular.

She looked very much like a woman who had only just given birth, her figure plumped, exaggerated, and yet he found he liked the look.

"I would apologize, but I'm not at all sorry. Have a seat." Breathing felt easier than it had a moment ago. He could only attribute it to Malik's exit.

She walked in slowly, blue eyes narrowed, glittering. "If you wanted to have dinner with me, all you had to do was tell me earlier."

"I don't *want* to have dinner with you, I need to discuss something with you," he said. "I thought it might be convenient to do it over dinner."

She blinked. "Oh. Well." She sat in a chair farther down the table and across from his.

"Come closer."

She scooted one chair over.

"Across from me," he said.

She rolled her eyes and stood, making her way down the table and taking the seat opposite him. "What exactly do we need to discuss?"

"We need to make sure there is paperwork that backs up our story. I would like to put you on payroll."

"I don't want money from you."

"Because you already got money?" He didn't bother to soften the words.

"I...that's..."

"Don't pretend you don't need it, you do. You admitted it was part of the reason you agreed to carry Aden in the first place."

"Yes. But I wanted to come here to care for him. I need to. I'm not going to accept money for…"

"While you are here, you can obviously have no other form of employment. In my mind that means you should be paid for your services."

She recoiled slightly, blue eyes wide. He didn't understand the woman. She had never once claimed she felt like she was Aden's mother, and it stood to reason, as she was not. Yet she seemed unable to part with him, and now unable to accept compensation for caring for him.

"I am going to set up an account in your name and I will deposit money into it as I see fit, no matter whether you agree to this or not." He needed her to take the money. Needed to put her in a neat, easily understood position, not simply for appearances, but for himself.

"Are you always like this?"

"Always. It is one of my more effective personality traits."

"It's one of your more impossible personality traits. Actually, I've only glimpsed this one personality trait in you. Do you have any more?"

"Not that I'm aware of. I get the job done, Chloe, that's who I am. I make sure everything works. That my people, my family, are safe and provided for. It's why you are here, for Aden's well-being."

"Fine. Set up an account."

"You aren't planning on taking anything out of it, are you?"

"I despise men like you," she said, her voice a low hiss. "You think you can just…control me. Take absolute…. You just think that you can buy someone. That you can own a woman simply because you have power and status and bigger muscles. It's not impressive. I see you exactly for what you are." She stood up, her frame trembling. He had no idea what had set her off, but he had a feeling it went deeper than a simple dinner invitation and a demand she take his money.

"A man making an attempt at protecting his family legacy?"

"A man who needs to…demonstrate his testosterone by posturing like an…animal," she spat.

Anger spiked through him, unreasonable, completely unusual. He should simply let her words slide off. But for some reason, they stuck into him like barbs, tore at his pride. Perhaps it was because he knew how wrong she was. That to be an animal, he would have to act with gut emotion. Intuition borne of feeling. And he possessed neither. The realization made him frighteningly, acutely aware of the void in him. The pit that seemed as though it could never be filled.

He felt poised on the brink of it. As if the tendrils of darkness reaching up for him might wrap themselves around him. Might drag him down into the abyss.

He stood, pushing his chair backward. "An animal? Is that what you think I am?"

"You've dragged me back to your lair."

"I brought you here," he growled, circling the long table slowly, his fingertips brushing the top of each chair he passed, "at your request."

All of the emotion, the intensity from the past few weeks, threatened to overwhelm Chloe. She was past the point of reason now. She was nothing more than a burning ball of kinetic energy, the forward motion unstoppable. She'd held it in for too long, let it build as she sat in her apartment, numbed by shock.

But the shock was gone now, and the trajectory of her emotions set. "Because I couldn't just let you take him!"

"I was hardly going to tear him from your arms." But he would have. They both knew it.

"But you were going to take him. As soon as possible."

"It's what needed to be done. It has nothing to do with you. None of this has anything to do with you," he said, his voice hard, simmering with barely contained anger. "You were the vessel. Nothing more."

She'd only ever felt the desire to hurt one other human being physically. Had only ever had to fight the urge to stop herself from attacking one other man. She'd never followed through on the feral, savage desire to hurt her father because she'd seen exactly what he could do with his fists. Had seen that he wouldn't hesitate to hit a woman. Not just once, but until she could no longer get back up.

But she didn't care about the consequences now.

She wanted to hit Sayid, with everything in her. Inflict pain on him for hurting her with his words. For telling the truth.

For saying that Aden was nothing more than her nephew, even though she'd carried him in her body. Given birth to him. In the big picture, it didn't matter. He wasn't hers and she had no claim on him. But spoken from that arrogant mouth, with such harshness, it was more than she could stand. The truth of it so raw and evident, so unwanted.

She stepped toward him without thinking, just as he rounded to her side of the table, her fist pulled back. He caught her arm, stopping her, tugging her up against him.

"You think you could hurt me?" he asked, his hand fitted securely around her arm without causing her any pain. His strength was so great, he didn't seem to be exuding any force. It only made her angrier. And now that the dam had burst on her control, she couldn't stop it all from pouring out.

"I might have been able to break your nose. It doesn't matter how much muscle you have, that's still a susceptible spot."

"If you think a broken nose would hurt me…you have a limited understanding of what I am capable of. Of what I have endured."

He lowered his head, dark eyes boring into hers. Heat bloomed in her stomach, her muscles quivering. He smelled like sandalwood, and clean skin, and there was no reason for her to notice something like that. No reason at all.

It wasn't the smell she usually associated with men. Her father was alcohol, sweat and tobacco. Occasionally, blood.

And as an adult, the only time she'd gotten close enough to a man to smell him was if they were sharing a microscope. And then he usually smelled like chemicals.

"If I release you, will you promise to put your claws back in?" he asked.

She shook her head. "Only if you watch what you say."

"Then we're at an impasse because I don't have to watch what I say."

"You're right," she said. "You do suck at diplomacy."

"I never claimed otherwise," he said, his tone rough.

"I don't have to like what you say. And I don't. Not at all."

"I'm not trying to hurt you," he said, his voice low. "But I am telling you the truth. I'm not going to wrap the situation up as something else and try to make it more palatable. It is an ugly situation. Nothing about it is simple." He released his hold on her and stepped back. "But we will survive it. As will Aden. If we do it right, he will thrive. This is about him. Not about us."

Her heart was thundering in her temples, her head

spinning. She put her hand over the place where his fingers had been. Her skin was hot, not to the touch, but beneath the flesh. Inside of her. She'd never felt anything like it before. Didn't understand how it was possible.

"On that we can agree," she said, aware, painfully, that she sounded breathless. That she was breathless.

"Then perhaps we can put a halt on the dramatics?"

"When you put a halt to your douche-baggery."

Dark brows locked together. "What is this word?"

"It means you're being a jerk. But more than a jerk even," she said. "Worse."

"No one talks to me like this," he said, his tone firm, not imperious. He was simply stating a fact, and she wasn't all that surprised by it. She didn't know why she felt empowered to speak to him like that. Maybe it wasn't empowerment so much as a need to push him away. Anger was safer than the pull she felt toward him. Much safer.

"No one who has any idea of how to act in polite company talks to people the way you do," she said.

"I spend a lot of time outside of polite company."

She crossed her arms beneath her breasts. "Clearly."

"Our discussion is through."

"What about dinner?"

"Suddenly, I am thinking I might take it in my room. Or an enemy prison. Either is preferable."

"You… You…"

"I will set up an account in your name. You will

be paid a generous salary. I will be meeting with the press tomorrow." A sudden rigidity came over him, his body tensing, his jaw tightening. "Aden will not be brought outside, but he will be in the smaller meeting room with the members of the media who possess special passes. You will hold him for the duration of the interview, but you will not speak."

"I will not speak?" she repeated, incredulous.

"No one will be asking questions about string theory which means it will not be necessary for you to do so. Now, you are dismissed."

"I am dismissed?"

"You keep repeating me. It wastes time."

"I'm…I can't believe you're…dismissing me."

"You didn't want to come and eat with me in the first place and now you're complaining that you don't have to?"

"Unbelievable."

"I concur."

She put her hands on her hips. "Not on the same thing, I don't think."

"Very likely not."

"Do I at least get dinner in my room?"

The look he gave her was almost comical in its seriousness. "No. It's bread and water for you, or nothing. Same as the rest of my staff. Didn't you know we're barbarians out here in the desert?"

"Be serious."

"I am. Be careful or you might wake up to find yourself leg-shackled to my bed."

It was as if a conduit had powered up between them, sparking to life and sending heat and energy on an invisible path between them. It held her in its thrall, forcing her to look into his eyes, dark, fathomless and magnetic. Completely and utterly compelling. And then it was as though the electricity had found a way beneath her skin, traveling along her veins, wrapping itself around each fiber in her body.

She couldn't look away, even though she wanted to—needed to.

And then the image he'd evoked suddenly hit her, clear as day. Her, tied to the bed, with his large, muscular body looking over her. Absolute strength. Absolute power. With her completely helpless, at the mercy of a man who possessed no tenderness.

A surge of fear overrode the strange electricity in her blood, snapped her out of her trance.

"You are…despicable," she spat.

"Perhaps I am," he said, dark eyes unchanging, unflinching. "I have been called a great many things, it's not inconceivable that some of them are true. It's very likely most of them are."

"It doesn't bother you?"

"Why should I care what anyone thinks? I was created to get results, no matter the consequence. I was not designed to win public favor, but to keep my people safe. By any means necessary. The grit to do that does not come from a beautiful place. Damn my image. It is worth nothing."

"But you…you're the leader now. Your job isn't the same as it was."

Black eyes turned to ice. "I am only the stop gap. I'm only here until Aden can step into his position. Not a moment longer."

"And what about Aden? You'll be his closest family. Will you…will you at least try to be decent for his sake?"

A shadow passed over Sayid's face, his expression horribly flat now. Dead. "The best thing for Aden would be if I stayed well away from him. And that is what I plan to do."

CHAPTER FOUR

"How did you not realize the child had survived?"

Sayid swallowed, looking out at the sea of people who sat, awaiting an explanation on how it was that an heir who had been lost to them, was now found.

Cold sweat beaded on his forehead, dripped down his back. The irony of it was not lost on him. He had looked into the cold eyes of death and had felt nothing, had stared down men with guns, dodged land mines on the battlefield, and he had felt nothing. No fear. No hesitation. But here looking down at the reporters, he felt cracks forming, felt something in him starting to break.

He was not a public speaker. He was not a man of words at all.

"There was much confusion following the death of my brother and his wife. The accident was...there were many people involved and it was not immediately made known to us that the sheikha had survived long enough to give birth."

"And is this the nanny?"

"Yes," Sayid said, focusing on a spot on the back

wall, not letting his focus stray to Chloe, or the tiny bundle she clutched in her arms. "Chloe was simply doing as instructed. Protecting the heir of Attar."

"A true heroine," said a female reporter in the back.

Sayid nodded, trying to come up with something to say, something that wasn't on the carefully planned script he'd gone over in his head, but his brain was moving slowly, words hard to grasp on to. "Chloe took a potential risk to her own safety to protect the child. She is indeed a heroine."

"And when will the heir be free to step into the position of ruler?" This from another reporter at the back.

Sayid gritted his teeth, fighting against the hostility burning in his veins. He craved the desert right then, the freedom of it. Craved the heat of the sun, the cleansing quality of it. It had the power to strip a man, burn away everything but that which was necessary.

Right now he felt as if he couldn't breathe, the walls closing down over him. "He must reach the age of majority before he can rule."

"Then is it to be understood that matters of national diplomacy will be handled by you until then, Sheikh?" asked one reporter, well-known for his rather antigovernment stance.

"There is no one else," Sayid said, the answer falling flat. "If there are no more questions, we are done here." He turned and stepped down from the podium, going to Chloe's side and placing his hand on her elbow, guiding her from the press room and into the corridor.

"The security guards will ensure the press stay put for the next fifteen minutes. I don't want them watching which wing of the palace we go to." That angle of the conference was straight in his mind, and he relished the return of control, of certainty.

Chloe looked at him, wide blue eyes strangely calm. Strange, because he felt like there was a live monster roaming around inside of his body and she had just passed through the same situation, yet looked unaffected. "You know a lot about security."

"That's as intelligent an observation as if I had said you know a lot about molecules. It is my duty. Who I am."

"I was giving you a compliment," she said, her tone stiff, "it won't happen again."

"It doesn't matter to me either way."

"You're a frustrating man."

"And you aren't the ideal woman, but here we are."

"You are…" Her cheeks turned pink, anger glittering in her eyes now. And it gratified him. Made him feel a sense of satisfaction that she wasn't quite so calm. "You are such an ass."

"You say that like you think I might care. Like I might be able to change it. I don't think you understand, Chloe, this is all there is to me."

She blinked slowly. She was upset now, he could

tell. And he found he liked it even less than her calm. "I have to go and study."

"And I'm certain that Malik can find more papers for me to sign. He finds my discomfort amusing, I think."

"Will I see you again today?"

He shook his head. "I should not think so. You won't require my presence, will you?"

"I shouldn't think so," she said, echoing his words.

"Good," he said, clipped. "Then I will go about my business, and you may go about yours."

Sayid turned away from Chloe, away from those unguarded eyes, and headed back toward his office. A tomb for the living, in his opinion. Each step sent a spike through his body, caused a subtle breaking inside.

He had told Chloe that the palace was preferable to prison. Today, he wondered.

"So soon? But you just promised me a reprieve."

Sayid looked at Chloe, perched at her desk, her red hair pulled back into a haphazard knot, black glasses framing, hiding, her eyes. "A reprieve from what?"

"Your presence. I'm doing course work." She looked away from him and back at the computer, but not before he noticed a dull flush of red staining her cheeks. It took a full second for his mind to process what that might mean, but his body had already reacted to it, blood rushing through his veins, hot, fast.

He shouldn't feel anything for her. Least of all for her blush. She was prickly. At best. If he tried to make a move on her she would likely freeze his cock off with a calculated stare.

It was the strangest thing, because she could be witty, evidence of a sly sense of humor and a brilliant mind. And she was a soft touch with Aden. But if he stepped over the invisible boundaries she'd set around herself and the little prince, she went on fullscale attack.

The memory of catching her arm as she tried to strike him, of pulling her soft body up against his, flashed through him.

No. He should not feel anything for her. He shouldn't feel anything full stop. But his defenses were down after the damned press conference. Cracks in his armor he had yet to repair. Control, impenetrable shields, were essential tools in his arsenal, and they did not work during press conferences. Did not work when addressing his people. Headlines about him were not kind. He lacked charisma, caring.

But he was at a loss as to how he was supposed to step into this new role while still clinging to the things his uncle had instilled in him, with rod and fist. Things that were, he knew, a matter of life and death.

He battled to get control over his body.

"Sorry," he said, matching the annoyance in her tone, portraying that he was most definitely not sorry. "There is a celebration happening in the streets in Aden's honor. In your honor."

She tugged her glasses off. "Mine?"

"Yes. Yours." Certainly not his. Chloe was the bright spot the country had been waiting for. She had brought the first bit of hope to Attar since the death of Rashid. Since Sayid's installation to the throne. "You are the savior of the heir of Attar. The savior, indirectly, of the country, and my people are celebrating."

"Except…I'm not the savior of anything. You lied."

"Did I?" He kept his eyes trained on her face, on her wide blue eyes. She looked vulnerable now, the anger, the extreme standoffishness, faded into the background. She was an interesting mix of softness and strength. And he didn't have time to be interested.

"Yes. You did. You made it sound like I wrested him from the claws of death or something, and the press seem to have believed you."

"You hid him until you could not hide him any longer, and I know that the bulk of your concern was for his safety, so the essence of the story remains the same. Had I given you instructions regarding his security, had there truly been suspicion surrounding the accident, I would have given you the same instructions. To hide him until we were certain he would be safe."

"I acted more out of shock than anything else."

"And fear of me," he said, watching her expression.

She stood, arching her back, her round breasts pushing against the stretchy cotton fabric of her top. His eyes were drawn there, his focus compromised. He was a man who liked women, a man who enjoyed sex. But he didn't let his desire off its leash unless it was an appropriate time. An appropriate woman. This was not the appropriate time. She was not the appropriate woman.

Which meant it was time to meet her eyes again, and not search for the outline of her nipples beneath the layer of thin fabric. But it was difficult to redirect himself. Much more so than it should have been.

He could see her swallow hard, her pulse pounding in her neck. He wanted to put his lips over that spot, taste her skin. "Well, can you blame me? The love of power is the inspiration for most of life's atrocities."

"Perhaps, but this," he said, sweeping his hand in front of him, indicating the palace, "is not the kind of power I crave."

She blinked. "And...what kind of power do you crave?"

"Simple," he said, his eyes blank. "I don't crave anything." A hard claim to make considering the current direction of his thoughts.

"That's impossible."

He shook his head. "Craving anything, in my position, would be dangerous. Something easily exploited."

She arched a pale brow, the expression of utter disbelief plain in her clear blue eyes. His eyes drifted lower again, to the curve of her full breasts, the intoxicating shape of her body.

"Everybody wants something," she said.

"I'm above such things."

It was almost impossible to keep himself from making a move toward her. It had been months since he'd been with a woman, time and circumstance not permitting it, and he was starting to feel the effects of his celibacy. But there was no time to deal with it now, and certainly not with her.

Another thing he needed power over. The strong, strange craving that was making its way through him, heating him from the inside out, making him burn. It was as if the Attari sun had penetrated his skin, as if cool blue eyes had the power to cover him in fire.

"High opinion of yourself."

"I am a sheikh," he said, "I expect to have a certain amount of power, as is my birthright. I was never the heir, but I have always been a leader. I ask for nothing. I demand it, and it is so."

A lie. Throughout his life, if he had demanded something that had not fallen into line with his uncle's vision for him, he had been denied it. Or it had been taken from him, ruthlessly.

He had spent years having any royal arrogance stripped from him, leaving him exposed. A man, simply a man, with no power but what he found inside of himself. No defense beyond the walls he built around his emotions. It had spurred him to make them stronger, to take everything his uncle had taught him and use it as a shield against those who sought to break him.

"I am the final authority," he said, reinforcing himself.

Her eyes shuttered, going cold and dim. "I see. Was there something you wanted or were you just informing me about the celebration?"

"Yes," he said, his voice getting rough, his body tightening in reaction to her words. He put his power into mastering it, into overcoming the inconvenient, unnecessary attraction to her that seemed to be intent on taking him over. "I came to issue you an invitation to the proceedings."

Unsurprisingly, "invitation" had meant that she was required to go. Aden was tucked safely in his bed, back at the palace with both of his nannies standing by.

And she'd had to put on the only dress that fit her and her newly expanded figure, again, and get into Sayid's limousine. Not that she had a direct complaint with the limo. Under any other circumstance, she would have thought it was really cool to ride in a limo. But his heavy-handed tactics, combined with the disturbingly close confines of the vehicle, were dampening her glee.

The fact that a car the size of this one gave the impression of close quarters said a lot about the disturbing effect Sayid seemed to have on her.

It was all that power, and the unapologetic enjoyment of it. He was so comfortable with it, so clearly in need of it. It made her fear what might happen if it was denied him. If he felt it was threatened.

What lengths would he go to in order to get it back?

Would he find it in the use of his fists against someone weaker than him? In a woman's pleading? Would he find it in holding the life or death of someone weaker than him in his hands?

Her father had. And while she knew that all men weren't abusers...men who prized power, men who were so unashamedly dominant, were the ones who set off her internal alarms.

And Sayid was certainly creating a strange effect in her. A kind of restless edginess. Nerves that cramped her stomach and made breathing difficult. A warning from her body, she was certain.

"See the hope they have now?" Sayid's voice was surprisingly soft.

Chloe looked out the window. It was no wild reverie that gripped the people lining the streets, rather a solemn expression of love for their country. Flowers in people's hands, a memorial for the fallen sheikh and his wife. A gift for the new prince.

"Yes," she said, her throat tight.

Sayid sat, his hands folded in his lap. The people outside waved, but Sayid made no move to wave back. Chloe pressed the button on the limousine window and expected to be scolded by Sayid. But he said nothing.

She slipped her hand outside the window and waved. The solemnity broke. Cheers erupted, smiles on the faces of the Attari people who before had looked so bereft. She looked at Sayid, questioning.

"You are the woman who saved their future ruler," he said. "You are loved."

"A strange thing to be loved for something you didn't do."

"You did save him, though," Sayid said, his tone strange, as though he was having a revelation even as he spoke. "You carried him. Gave him life. You're the reason he is."

"If not me, it would have been someone else."

"But it was you."

Yes, it had been. And now the whole thing was tearing her apart slowly, piece by painful piece. Because her plan for her life had been so perfect. And she'd been so happy with it. Now it was altered forever.

She could never again find the same satisfaction in her imaginings of the future. There was a time when the thought of being Dr. Chloe James had filled her with all the satisfaction she could ever ask for from life. When picturing her own classroom filled with students had seemed like the ultimate picture of fulfillment. Spending her days lecturing on what she loved, spending time studying as much as possible even after school, unraveling new theories, either proving or disproving them as they came. There was a time when that had been more than enough.

And now it was muddled. Because to have that, she had to push Aden out of the picture. The thought of it sent a sharp pain through her, a spear lodged in her breast, one she couldn't seem to pull out.

And the thought of abandoning the dream was painful, too.

There was no simple answer. There was just the reality of being caught between two different worlds. Two different desires.

But of course, she couldn't stay in Attar. Couldn't be staff at the palace forever.

Which still gave her her dream, that wonderful fantasy she'd clung to since she was thirteen years old.

Except now it was tarnished. It would never again be the vision of utter contentment and perfection it had once been. Not now that it meant giving up so much.

She was changed. Completely. And she hated it. Resented it with every fiber of her being. Yet, she couldn't feel any resentment toward Aden. Toward the life that had begun inside of her body.

It was easier to channel it to Sayid. Much easier.

"The people need a symbol," he said, his tone

grave. "I am not that symbol. No hope for the future. You…you bring hope."

"It's Aden," she said.

"Yes, it is. But it's you, too. You who brought them their king. Who risked my wrath, and believe me my wrath is legendary, to save him."

"I didn't think it would cost nearly so much," she said, her throat tightening.

"And was it not worth it?" he asked, his tone hard. As if he had any right to judge her, while he sat there, power pouring off of him in waves.

The anger bubbled over. Again. She was normally so much better with control, but Sayid tested her. And after being alone in her struggle, in her pain, for weeks, she simply couldn't stand keeping it all in anymore.

"You…you—" she pulled her hand back in the window "—you can sit there and act so superior to me? You have the power to move Aden and me around like pawns on a chessboard, and frankly, you have from the moment you walked into my apartment. And then you just…say things like that. As though this is all so clear-cut and I'm supposed to know exactly how to feel, exactly what to say and want. It's easy for you. You have all the control. And beneath the control…you don't care. You don't have a single feeling, not one sliver of emotion. So of course this is easy for you. Of course it's clear-cut. But unlike you, I have a heart, and that makes all of this incredibly confusing. Incredibly painful. Don't you dare presume that you should know what I feel when you don't feel a damn thing."

Her voice was trembling when she finished, her words unsteady, tears threatening. But she wouldn't let them fall. Wouldn't let him see how vulnerable she felt. How raw. How perilously close she was to cracking apart.

Sayid only looked at her, his expression unchanging. He was unmoved. A man made of stone instead of flesh.

Finally, he spoke. "Easy?" he asked. "You think this is easy? Look at them, Chloe. At best they fear me, at worst, they are ashamed to have a man like me in power. A man of violence. There is nothing easy here."

"You always seem so calm."

"I am trained to." He was silent for a moment. "You were wrong about something else."

"What else, Sayid?"

"I do not see Aden as a pawn. He is king, and I will do everything in my power to protect him."

"And what about me?" she asked, the words sticking to the sides of her throat.

"Every other piece is incidental," he said, uncompromising. Unfeeling. "Life is war, and the only thing that matters is the checkmate. Not how many pieces you lose on the way. If the king isn't standing in the end, all is lost." Dark eyes met hers, the intensity of it, the visceral reaction his expression set off in her stomach, frightening. "Everything else, everyone else, is expendable."

CHAPTER FIVE

FOR THE NEXT COUPLE OF weeks, Sayid simply wasn't around. And Chloe was grateful for it. His words, callous, and clearly true to him, had put her on guard.

She was nothing but a pawn to him. Simply an incidental. If scandal threatened to break, he would ship her back to Portland, of that she was certain. And she wasn't ready to leave Aden.

Not yet.

She had nearly six months left with him, and she was going to treasure every moment. Capture it so she could hold it close. Always.

She closed her eyes and envisioned her hypothetical classroom again. It would be filled with students ready to learn.

And in the back of her mind, she would wonder the whole time about Aden. If he was being held enough. Loved enough.

She stood up from her computer and tugged her glasses off, walked from her room into his. She knew she shouldn't pick him up since he was sleeping, but after the jarring thought of being separated from him, thousands of miles between them, she needed closeness. Needed to feel the bond that had been growing, strengthening, since the moment she first felt him move inside of her.

While pregnant, she'd never thought of him as hers. But it had been impossible not to marvel at it. She knew all about the development of babies in the womb. Such an intricate act of science that required everything to happen according to a perfect plan, with precision, with timing that was utterly essential.

And it had been happening inside of her.

Then, when he'd been born, all she'd thought about was survival. Hers and his. A bond forged by fire.

Now…it was changing again. When she thought of him, everything inside of her softened, the emotion she felt was an ache that started at the base of her throat and spread throughout her chest, to her limbs. And there was no rational explanation she could find for it, no biological excuse to try and explain it away.

Because biologically, Aden wasn't her son. But her body had stopped caring.

Her heart didn't care very much anymore, either. But her brain…her brain knew. Knew that it couldn't last. That he wasn't hers. That the wise decision was to keep aiming for her academic and professional ideal.

That this interruption of her plan, this detour, shouldn't be allowed to matter so much.

For the first time, her brain was losing the argument.

She reached into the crib and picked Aden up. He squeaked, burrowing into her chest, the little noise making her heart lift. What was she doing? She wasn't mother material. She knew nothing about a functional mother-child relationship.

And she wasn't his mother.

You're the only one he has.

That her brain knew and agreed with. There would be no nurturing from Sayid. There would be nothing from his uncle, no affection, no kissing scraped knees. There would be staff.

The thought of it chilled her, down to that deep, indefinable part of herself that was made up of pure, raw emotion. The part that transcended logic and reason. Trumped it completely.

She couldn't allow it.

Certainty spread through her, a certainty that had been growing, steadily and surely, since the moment Aden was born.

She didn't want to walk away from her life in Portland. Didn't want to put her dreams on hold.

But she could.

The one thing she couldn't do was walk away from Aden.

"Sayid, I need to speak with you."

Sayid looked up and saw Chloe standing in the doorway. She was wearing black slacks, a white button-up shirt and a suit jacket. The buttons on the white top gapped at her breasts and the jacket was left unbuttoned, likely too tight for her post-baby figure.

He needed to have his dresser get her a new wardrobe that would accommodate her curves, but he hadn't had the time. Especially because he'd been so busy avoiding her. Doing necessary work, of course, but avoiding her had been a perk.

"It's far too hot for that outfit," he said.

"Yes," she said, wiping a hand over her forehead, "but appropriate for a meeting."

"You've called a meeting with the sheikh, have you?" He pressed his palms flat against the cool surface of the desk. "Ambitious. But I am very busy."

"It concerns your king," she said, her tone icy enough to leave frost on his desk in spite of the desert sun that blazed outside. His body reacted to it, a visceral response that went deep. His attraction to her was completely unexplainable. He liked women unchallenging and biddable. Liked women who wanted a couple hours and orgasms of his time and nothing more.

Sex was perfunctory for him. Another need that he saw was met. It wasn't this. This…desire that was turning itself into an ache. That filled in the cracks that were starting to break open inside of him and forced them deeper, wider.

"Then speak, but be quick." He curled his fingers in slowly, making fists, using the tension to help combat the tightening in his gut.

"Six months is no longer agreeable for me," she said, clipped.

The desire that had been pooling in his gut, wearing a gully through the stone wall that blocked his emotion, turned into rage. It was far too late to stop the flow by the time he realized what he'd allowed to escape.

"Cutting into your study time is he?" Sayid asked, keeping his voice measured, keeping his emotions in check. He couldn't credit what made him so angry about her announcement. Couldn't credit why he'd allowed himself to feel it.

Everything was in place for Aden's care. Chloe was an incidental. An incidental that was popular with the people, but an incidental nonetheless. He didn't need her and neither did Aden.

Yet the idea that she could be so callous as to abandon her baby... No. Not her baby. Rashid and Tamara's baby. Chloe had no reason to stay and he would do well to remember that.

"Not in the least," Chloe said, her answer surprising him.

"I will not argue with you, Chloe. You were the one who asked to come, if you would like to leave now, the door is wide-open. Aden will want for nothing. Considering the experience, or lack of it, that you bring to the table, I doubt Aden will miss you too terribly."

"Is that what you think?" she asked, her tone thick.

"I do." He looked back down at the paperwork on

his desk. "Shall I ready the private plane to take you back to the States?"

He heard her take a deep breath in. "No, actually, what I was trying to tell you was that six months is no longer enough for me. I need more."

"What more do you need?" he asked.

"It's never going to be enough," she said. "Ever. I thought it would. I thought if I waited, then I would really start to long for the future I always imagined I would have. And I still want it, it's not that I don't, it's just that…it's not the most important thing anymore, and no matter how hard I try to make it the most important thing, I can't."

"What exactly do you mean?" His patience was getting short.

"Aden," she said, her voice raw. "I don't know what I'm doing with him, but at this point, I know one thing. I can't…leave him. Not in six months, not ever. I tried to be rational about it, and tell myself that he's not my son. Tell myself I've worked too hard for too long to compromise my position in graduate school but I…"

"What are you proposing?" he bit out.

"That I stay."

"For how long?"

"For…for forever?"

"You intend to stay here in the palace—in Attar—forever?"

"It's not ideal, I grant you that. I'm much more suited to the climate in Portland, and I was going to school there. And I miss trees, dammit. But… but not nearly as much as I'll miss Aden if I leave. I can't leave."

"This is what you want?"

She shook her head, looking down at the floor. "I don't know what I want anymore. I spent most of my life wanting one thing, and now it just doesn't mean what it did anymore. Now I don't know what I want. All I know is what I can live without, and what I can't."

"And how is it I'm to explain to the world that Aden's life-saving nurse can't bear to leave him?"

"Sounds plausible to me," she said. "You know how we women are with our emotions, and other nonsense sheikhs just don't bear."

"There's a chance it will cause suspicion and that's one thing we can't have."

"Why?" she asked, weak. Pitiful. She was showing her vulnerability. He could crush her now, emotionally, as easily as he could crush her if he wrapped his fingers around her soft, lily-white throat.

The showing, so artless, so genuine, sent a shock of anxiety through him. Didn't she know what people could do with such an open expression of emotion? How much power it gave to others? She had just given him a weapon capable of destroying her, one that would enable him to manipulate her into doing whatever he chose.

She had revealed her biggest weakness to a man who had been trained to exploit weakness in others.

To use it with ruthless precision. He both rejoiced in it, and feared for her.

Now the decision he had to make was what he would do with it. If anything.

"You know why," he said, keeping his tone calm, collected. "It's not just to preserve the memory of Rashid and Tamara, it's so that Aden's right to the throne is never contested. DNA testing is fine and good, but can you imagine what the more traditional citizens of my country would think about you carrying the sheikha's child? If he is perceived to be illegitimate, or the product of something unnatural, then the way they view their future king could be compromised and I will not allow it."

"Protect the king," she said. "At all costs."

"Otherwise the game is lost."

Chloe took a shaky breath, feeling outside of herself, as if she was above her body somewhere, watching, rather than living in the moment.

"There has to be a way. There has to be…"

"Six months was the agreement, Chloe," he said, his voice hard. "Anything beyond that cannot be guaranteed."

"I see." She heard herself answer, but she wasn't sure if she spoke the truth. Or how she'd managed to get the words out past the lump in her throat.

"It is not my intention to hurt you, but I have to think of Attar. Of Aden."

"I am thinking of Aden."

"In a sense, yes. But I am thinking of his future

as a ruler, not of his need to be tucked in at night. I'm thinking of the essential things."

She wanted to argue that being tucked in at night was essential. At least, she imagined that it was. Her mother had been too caught up in the husband who used and mistreated her to take time for her daughter. And her father… She had started shrinking away from his touch at an early age, her survival instinct screaming that he was a predator who saw those smaller and weaker as prey. She'd retreated into her mind, found comfort there, because there had never been anything physical for her to find comfort in.

But she imagined it could be essential. That it could be wonderful.

"There's more to life than duty," she said.

"Not when you're royalty, *habibti,* not then. Because the happiness, the future, of millions of people depend on you. A royal is both the most important person in a country, and the least. For they must give it all in the name of serving the people."

Her stomach clamped down hard. "I don't want that for him."

"It is what he was born for."

"I know."

"Then you cannot stand in the way of it." He looked back down at his paperwork, and she could tell by his posture that he was through with her.

She was through with him, too. For now. She wasn't letting go of the idea. The certainty that she was asking for the right thing by asking to stay with

Aden had only grown when he'd refused her. If there was one thing she knew how to do, it was put her head down and soldier on, no matter how hard things were.

No matter how violently the storm raged around her, she knew how to keep herself safe. How to keep herself from going crazy. Even with everything happening in her home growing up she'd gotten perfect grades in school. She'd learned to insulate herself, to go to her mind, to ignore what seemed like impossibilities and find ways to work around them.

The only absolutes were in the scientific world, and she'd made it her business to discover them all. Everything else had room for negotiation.

She turned on her heel and walked out of Sayid's office. Yes, she was done with him for now. Until she could formulate a plan. And once she did, heaven help the man that thought he could control her, put her in her place as easily as he seemed to think he could.

It had been several hours since his confrontation with Chloe, and Sayid had spent that time going over the news stories that had been written about Aden and the circumstances surrounding his birth. And the stories written about him. The uncertainty, the doubt in his ability to do anything more than use brute force to get results.

Chloe James was hailed as a hero. The woman who had risked the wrath of the remaining royal family in order to ensure the safety of their miracle child.

There was speculation as well of who would be raising the beloved heir. It was rumored, and it was true, that an army of staff and nannies would be on hand to deal with the child. And concern over what sort of influence Sayid would be able to provide. If he would show Aden anything other than the cold stone wall he presented to the media.

He was a symbol of Attar's strength. Of its unbending attitude to its enemies. And his country knew it. He made such a success of the image that even his own people feared him.

The media wanted a family for their beloved prince. One that would fill the void left by Rashid and Tamara. And one thing they were certain about: Sayid could not fill that void.

But Chloe James could.

Oh, she was no natural mother, anyone could see that. But there was a need there, a fierce protectiveness that was unlike anything he'd ever seen. Even more than that, the nation recognized her as Aden's savior, and by extension, theirs.

As dark as the loss of Rashid had been, it had been even bleaker still that he was the one left to rule. There were whispers of his incompetence, even throughout the palace. That he was too hard. Too damaged from his years away from the palace, his time as a prisoner of war.

The second son's duty was to serve the country.

Not simply as a soldier, but as the lead military strategist. Second sons were sent away to learn, to cultivate toughness and strength. Second sons could not afford to be treated with softness or affection.

The need for empathy was a necessary trait for a leader, but not for a man of war. A machine of war.

His uncle, the second son of his family, had raised Sayid for most of his life. A man who had seen much war, a man who had lived through things no man should live through. A man who had emerged with his sanity and who had set out to make sure Sayid was strong enough to do the same.

You are a symbol for the country, Sayid. An ideal. An ideal must never be allowed to fail, or everyone who puts faith in it will fail along with it.

So he had become more than a man. And in so doing he had lost his humanity. Something that didn't bother him anymore. That required feeling. Feeling he didn't have.

It had been Kalid who had taken that final weakness, that final bit of tenderness inside of him, and given him reason to cut it out of his chest on his own. It had seemed a cruelty then. Pain beyond measure. But the man had been showing him his own weakness, and showing him why it must not be allowed to remain in him.

Look at how your weakness betrays you.

So he had carved all of the emotion, the empathy, the love, the pain, from his chest, leaving it hollow. Leaving himself protected. Leaving others protected.

But Aden was born to be a leader. His requirements were different. His needs were different.

It was not in Sayid to admit weakness, and yet, in this area, there was no circumventing it. He was at a loss to provide love, emotional support, to the future heir of his country.

He picked up one of the newspapers from his desk, the one with Chloe's picture on the cover, of her standing behind him, a blanket-wrapped bundle in her arms.

They were positioned just as the royal family would have been positioned for a press conference, with her to his right, just behind him, the child in her care.

It could not have been posed better if they were trying to make it appear that that was what they were: a family.

His brain began to quickly slot things into place. Turning problems to solutions was a major part of his life, of how he kept people safe. And yes, he had failed in it before, but he had sworn he never would again.

Just a few hours ago, the desire Chloe James felt to stay in Attar was a problem. A slow smile, one that had nothing to do with happiness, curved his lips upward.

He knew just how to make Chloe a solution.

CHAPTER SIX

STRATEGY WAS IMPORTANT when it came to doing battle with the enemy. Whether the enemy was a super soldier, hell-bent on destroying you and your people, or a petite redhead with an affinity for whiteboards.

Yes, strategy was always important.

Sayid surveyed the room, lined with heavy wooden bookshelves that were now filled with books pertaining to physics and other sciences. There were work spaces, a large table put there expressly for the purpose of spreading several of the large, shelved books out onto its surface. A desk in the corner with a new laptop docked to a large monitor on it. And whiteboards. Whiteboards, he knew, were a key point in this tactical maneuver.

Where most rooms in the palace spoke of the old world, this one was sleek, modern and filled with every convenience Chloe could ever ask for.

Ultimately, this little show of bribery was just to make things easier. He knew what Chloe would say already. Knew it because she had shown her hand.

Had revealed to him just how important staying was to her.

He had followed every rule of combat to the letter. He had found the weakness, he had taken hold of the power, and now he was ready to exploit it.

"You wanted to see me?"

Chloe walked into the room, scanning her surroundings slowly. Her movements were slow. Cautious. Suspicious. Good. Perhaps she was a bit more savvy when it came to protecting herself than he'd given her credit for.

He found it more of an asset than he might have thought. But then, the sheikha of Attar would have to be savvy. Particularly when she was living a lie.

"Yes," he said, "I did."

"In regard to?"

"Your request earlier."

"The one you flatly denied?"

"The very one. I had some time to reconsider."

She clasped her hands in front of her. She looked very pale, her frame delicate, small. But there was steel in her eyes, a strength he had underestimated. His mistake. She had shown her steel. The way she'd kept Aden, cared for him, concealed him out of concern for his safety.

Sayid had seen the emotion as pure weakness, but there was steel beneath it. Still, the depth of her caring for Aden put her at his mercy, and he would not hesitate to use his position to get what he wanted.

"And *have* you reconsidered?" she asked.

"As it happens, I have."

She froze for a moment, total shock evident on her face. "You have?"

He nodded. "You were right. Aden needs more than I can give him. I'm not someone who is going to spend time in the nursery. Not the type of man who would ever throw a ball around in the garden with a child. I'm not going to get excited over poorly drawn pictures or hang finger paintings on the wall in my office, and I will not insult you by pretending otherwise."

"Is this supposed to be encouraging in some way?"

"I am," he said, walking toward her, "acknowledging that your help will be needed in Aden's upbringing."

Chloe's knees started shaking and she gripped the back of one of the plush chairs in front of her to keep from revealing it. "That's…good."

"I thought you would see that."

"Of course I do, I suggested it."

Sayid's dark eyes met hers. "In a sense. But the situation, the concerns, I pointed out earlier have not changed. If we are to ensure that the fiction of Aden's birth remains intact, then there are certain safeguards we need in place."

"What kind of safeguards?" She didn't like his tone. It was so smooth, so practiced, and beneath it, a layer of darkness that seemed to coat her, make her tremble with fear and something more. Something she couldn't put a name to. Something she didn't want to put a name to.

She hated that it was his darkness that compelled her so. That his darkness drew her, a black flame that she wanted to touch, even knowing what the outcome would be. This was why she'd always avoided men. Why she'd never had a relationship.

"The press has made it plain that they do not think I am fit to raise Aden. Rashid and I were hardly raised by our own parents. Though, Rashid more than I. I rarely lived in the palace, my education taking me elsewhere, my uncle Kalid taking the largest portion of responsibility for my upbringing. However, Rashid married a Western woman. One who had already started changing the way things were done, breaking down the formal social constructs that existed for a thousand years. And no one was sorry to see them go."

"Tamara would have never let Aden out of her sight, much less out of the palace to be handled only by staff."

"Precisely."

"That's one reason it's so important for me to stay. To honor her wishes."

"With all respect for my late sister-in-law, who, though you might find this hard to believe, I had a great deal of admiration for, it is not her wishes that concern me."

"No?"

"No. Have you seen what they write about me?" he asked.

"Who?"

"The reporters. The Attari news, the world news. Have you seen?"

"No."

"Man without a heart, they say. A man with no skills in negotiation. One who will make Attar look like nothing more than a military country, lacking in the kind of diplomacy that is so essential in this age. They hate me, Chloe. And under such circumstances, how can I lead?"

"Maybe you should smile more."

He affected the expression. "That would help, you think?"

She looked at him and grimaced. "No. You still don't look very friendly."

"It cannot continue."

She knew he didn't mean the smile. "I didn't think you cared about your image."

"I don't. But if this continues, if we start to look too frayed to the outside world...we will become vulnerable to it. We must present a front of absolute unification for our enemies. If there is dissent from within, we will rot from within, and rest assured, the countries we share borders with will happily take advantage of our weakness and watch us crumble."

He spoke with ferocity, intensity, his dark eyes boring into hers.

"And how do you propose to do that?" she asked,

knowing as soon as she asked the question that she wasn't going to like the answer.

"I intend to propose," he said, cold humor twisting his lips into a smile that held no warmth or hint of happiness.

"What exactly do you mean by that?"

"It's very simple, Chloe James. I intend to take you as my wife."

Chloe felt as if she'd been punched in the stomach, all the air leaching from her body, making her gasp. "What?"

"Not a real wife, you understand. This is about presenting the image of a family to the people. If I am meant to raise Aden as my own, my wife will be expected to treat him as her own. You want to stay, you want that role, so I am giving it to you."

"But…you want me to marry you?"

"I don't want you to marry me, I want to protect Aden and give the people what they expect, give them an image that will bring comfort."

Chloe felt as though her heart was trying to claw its way up her throat. Failing that, she was certain it would beat through her chest. She knew all about marriage. About the dynamic between a husband and wife. About what a man did when he saw a woman as his property.

She knew that not every man was abusive. That not every marriage was marked by violence. She knew it, but in her head, it was all she could see.

The word *husband* brought forward visions of her

father venting his rage on her mother, the woman laying on the floor as he continued to hit her. Kick her. And on the wall behind them was their wedding portrait, the bride in white, smiling lovingly at the man who was now trying to wring the life out of her with his hands.

It was a vision that was with her always, this scene of extreme violence and suffering. It was, now and forever her strongest association with the words *husband* and *wife*.

"We won't have to stay married forever."

"Just until Aden assumes the throne?" she asked, her tone incredulous.

"Yes. Just until then."

"So only sixteen years of my life spent married to a man that I don't even like?"

"I'm spending sixteen years in a position that I don't want, until Aden is ready to rule. I understand that this isn't your country, that your loyalty isn't the same as mine. But your loyalty is to Aden, isn't it? To giving him what your sister wanted him to have?"

Her heart felt as if it was being torn in two. Visions of her future burning before her, turning to ash and floating away on the wind. And she had to let them burn, along with her fear, because the only other option was leaving Aden behind. Visiting when she could, and otherwise going on with her life as though it hadn't changed forever.

She couldn't do that. Had come to that conclusion already.

"Does it have to be marriage? I am Tamara's half sister. I'm Aden's aunt. It's entirely possible that I would move into the palace for those reasons alone."

"For a while, yes. But until he's a grown man?"

"Well, I don't consider sixteen a grown man…"

"In Attar it is different," he said, his tone hard and cold as ice.

If she left, this was Aden's family. His closest family. There would be no warmth from his uncle.

"It would just be a legal marriage, right?"

He nodded once. "I have no desire for a wife. And it is traditional for the royal couple to have separate quarters."

"Rashid and Tamara didn't."

"They were unusual. Theirs was a love match, and Tamara's American sensibilities colored the way they did things."

"Rashid never struck me as being very traditional."

"He wasn't. It was one reason he gravitated to Tamara."

"But we…"

"We will be a traditional Attari couple. It will be no hardship. In fact, it will come as little surprise that you're the woman I select as my queen. You demonstrated bravery, the desire to protect Aden at all costs. Love is not always a factor in marriages here, particularly not royal marriages. No one will expect it."

Chloe swallowed hard, the earlier image of her parents branded in her mind. "Can I think about it?"

"Of course." He looked at her as though he expected thinking about it would only take a few moments of her time.

"Not with you watching me."

"It is quite clear-cut. The only thing you're finding difficult is your emotional connection to the idea of marriage. And I have no such emotional idea. About marriage or anything else."

"I'm sure you don't. But it's not just that…" She looked up at him, his eyes boring into hers, gripping her, holding her. Stealing her words.

"You'll be able to finish your schooling. I spoke to the president of the university about you continuing on in your studies from Attar, and I provided you with this space so that you could work easily."

Anger came to her rescue, demolishing the fear, demolishing the strange attraction that seemed to pull her to him. "You…you what?"

"There is no need to thank me."

"I'm not going to thank you! You called the president of the university? And you told him I would be completing my studies from here without even speaking to me?"

"You told me you wanted to stay already."

"And you told me no."

"And I changed my mind when I found the solution to the problem."

Chloe felt as if her head might explode. "But I didn't agree to anything."

"Naturally, Chloe, we both know you will say yes. You want to be with Aden and this is the most practical way to go about it. This is the best thing. The best way for me to keep the nation whole, intact until Aden takes the throne."

"You don't know that I'll say yes," she said.

"Yes, I do. And when I told Dr. Schultz that you were staying here to marry me and become the sheikha of Attar he was naturally very supportive."

"You told him I was going to marry you?" She put her hands on her face and started pacing. "Oh...I'm going to have a stroke."

"No, you aren't."

Her head snapped back up. "Oh? I'm not? Well, I guess you would know since you seem to know exactly what I'm going to do at all times. Do you have any more brilliant insights into me for me? Oh, all powerful Sheikh, please reveal to me, the poor, little, feebleminded woman, my desires."

"You are being overdramatic now, Chloe."

"I am not. I am being exactly as dramatic as the situation demands."

"What is the difference between you living here in a room in the palace, and you living here in a room in the palace with a title and a marriage certificate? Practically, for you, there will be very little difference."

"Marriage honestly means nothing to you?"

"It is nothing more than a social construct. Without emotion or obligation to remain faithful, why should it mean anything? I do not want a wife, and you certainly won't be filling the position. You will be here for Aden, which will be to your benefit. And you will be here for public events, which, I will not lie, will be for mine. But I will require nothing from you in terms of what a man wants from a wife. I don't need a place in your bed, neither do I wish for you to give me children."

"Good, because I don't want that stuff, either." She ignored the little kick that went through her body at the mention of being in bed together. Ignored it so well it was almost as if it hadn't happened. Because it didn't mean anything. Nothing at all. "I can't believe you. You arrogant, controlling…"

"Decisive," he finished. "I am decisive. You said what you wanted and I set out to find a solution that would work. More than work, I have found one that will benefit us both. I suggest you thank me, rather than verbally abusing me."

"I think your ego can stand it."

"I don't have an ego, Chloe. I see things as they are, as they need to be in order to work. It's not about ego, it's about knowing my place in life and ensuring that I meet every obligation. I will do it for Aden and when you are my wife, I will do it for you."

When, not *if.*

Chloe felt as though she was breaking apart inside. Like the world, the world she knew anyway, had cracked and was shattering around her, taking away any sense of certainty, any idea of where the right path was.

She was standing in the dark, wishing she had a lantern so she could find her way.

But she had a feeling there was no right way. Not now. There was only the way that would hurt the least, the way she could best manage.

If only she knew for certain which direction that was. Because one choice would lead her back to Oregon, back to her life as she'd planned it since she was a teenager. But it would lead her away from Aden.

And the other way would lead her straight into the lion's den. Straight into the thing she feared the most.

But she would be here. Would be with her child.

And he really could be hers. No more holding herself slightly at a distance to keep herself from breaking.

She swallowed, fear, grief, making her throat tight, making it hard to breathe.

And in the darkness, she saw the light. It came with an image of Aden. Because in that instance she realized that out of every desire she had, that one would never lessen. The connection with him would never fade.

Jobs would change, what she wanted in terms of work would change. The people in her life would come and go. She would move out of her apartment, and lose her attachment to the old one. She would complete her doctorate and find new, more challenging goals.

But no matter what changed in that part of her life, no matter where her priorities shifted to, her love for Aden would remain. It would be the constant, no matter what she was surrounded by. And if she chose to leave, the grief, the pain at being separated, would be the companion to that love.

She couldn't bear it. Couldn't bear the idea of embracing ephemeral, temporary things for the one connection she had that had ever felt real. Permanent. For the only family she had.

It was more than even that now, more than just a desire for her family. Aden was her son. No matter what the truth might be genetically, the truth of her emotions was that he was nothing other than her own child.

"All right, Sayid, I will marry you," she said, the words getting stuck in her throat.

There was no look of victory on his face, no sense of triumph, just a single nod, his expression remaining as cold and unreadable as ever. "And I will have it arranged. The sooner the better."

He turned and strode from the room, leaving her standing there, surrounded by books and whiteboards. That at least was a familiar comfort.

A part of her had always feared marriage, but in that vision, she'd been weak. Clinging to the man she called husband, as her mother had done.

No, that wouldn't be her life. Because in order

for a man to have that kind of power over her, she would have to love him. And she didn't love Sayid. She never would.

More than that, he would never feel any passion toward her.

There was no emotion in him, and in that there was safety.

Sayid was as cold as ice. And she welcomed that. Clung to the safety in his lack of emotion.

As long as there was no passion, there would be no danger.

CHAPTER SEVEN

SAYID RAN, THE SAND HOT even through his shoes. The sun was a punishment, sending heat through his skin and into his body, burning him from the inside out, cleansing him.

He stopped and looked around him. There was nothing visible in any direction, the slight hill behind him concealing the palace from view. And everywhere else…there was simply nothing. Nothing but open space. Red sand. Bleached sky. No walls. No bars.

Even so, it felt as if chains were tightening on his wrists, binding him, squeezing his throat, threatening to crush his windpipe. He had nightmares at night, every night, of the blackness. Of being bound, unable to move. Of waiting. Waiting for the crack of the whip, the blade of a knife, over flesh.

Waiting for pain he couldn't show he felt. Crushing the agony down, turning it inward so that no one would ever know how close he was to being broken.

He bent at the waist, his hands braced on his knees as he tried to block out that feeling of being trapped, the sense of walls closing in on him. Usually, being out in the Attari desert helped. The vast openness, the sense of unending space relieving the dark claustrophobia that lived inside of him.

This time it didn't stop. He felt trapped, felt as though he couldn't breathe.

He sat down, uncaring that the sand burned his legs where his shorts exposed them to the elements, not caring that the sun beat down on him with all the cruelty of a whip.

He felt as if he would burst, his breath coming slow and hard, pressure building inside of him, rage, so strong, so uncontrollable that he had to let it out. Only here. Only with the desert as witness.

Only here could he allow himself to feel the crushing weight of all that had been placed on him at birth. There had been chains on him long before he'd been taken prisoner. Chains put on him, first by his family, by the expectation that came with being the son meant to oversee the military, meant to oversee the protection of a nation. By all he'd been forced to give up, held captive to the life he'd been born into.

But in the end, he kept the chains of his own free will. He had tightened them. In that prison cell, the one that had stolen a year of his life, he had suffered indignity. Had lived in filth, had been stripped naked, every sign of rank and stature stolen. And then the skin had been stripped from his body.

But the harder they had pressed, the stronger he'd made his walls. The greater the weight, the deeper he buried his pain. He was the symbol of the strength of his nation and no matter how hard he was pushed, he knew he could never break.

Knew he could never allow weakness, emotion, to come in and crack the walls. That torture, the captivity, was the time in his life he'd been created for. Was the reason he had been broken, then remade, in his youth.

He had taken beatings already, had already lost all he'd cared about. At the hands of his uncle. The only family involved in his daily life. But it had been necessary.

And then Rashid had died. And another weight had been added to him. More defenses had needed to be built. And the man had been buried deeper still. But it was no longer a refuge, not like it had been during his time with his uncle, or in the enemy prison. Now it threatened to choke him.

In that moment, the need to break free of it, the need to scream into the silence of the desert, to release the tension that was threatening to crush him in its grip, was overwhelming. But he could not. He was too tightly bound.

Now he would have a wife. A child.

A chance he'd thought lost to him. A chance he no longer wanted. Not anymore.

Another woman. Another time. Another baby. One that had never been allowed to take its first breath.

And Sura...

Sayid's love for her had been unacceptable, his loss of control with her a weakness. And that was why, at sixteen, his uncle had ensured that the woman who held Sayid's heart had been given to another.

Sayid could remember still, watching the armored car that carried her driving away. Taking her to the home of her future husband.

But she's pregnant. The baby...

There is no pregnancy now, Sayid. Her father ensured that it was dealt with. And Sura is to be married to another.

Who? Where?

It is not your concern. She is not for you. She never could be. It is not what you were meant for.

He had longed to cut his own heart out in that moment, would have done it, gladly, because the pain would have been preferable to the loss, unending, searing, that he had felt then. He had been on his knees, broken.

Do you see, Sayid? Do you see the power she had? The power it would have given to your enemies? They would have used her against you. You cannot love like that. To feel like that, is to give your power to others.

Kalid had been right. Then, as ever. Had shown him the power such a weakness might give his enemies. And Sayid had taken the final step that day, purging himself of every emotion, leaving nothing more than the ideal he had been born to be. A symbol of the nation. Untouchable. Immovable.

He had given up on the thought of having a wife. Of having a child.

But Chloe would not be his wife. Not truly. And Aden would never be his child. Nothing had changed. Nothing would change.

He stood, carefully closing himself down again, shutting the doors against all the feeling he had just released, against the pain, against the feeling of being in bondage.

And the chains on his soul loosened, a numbness taking their place.

By the time he returned to the palace, he felt nothing again.

"Thankfully, we will be spared the circus that often comes with a royal wedding," Sayid said, his eyes connecting with hers across the table.

He had requested, with some advance notice even, that she join him for dinner that evening. Everything in her had rebelled against the idea but she really couldn't afford to follow the feeling. They didn't have to play like a love-struck couple, but she could hardly seem afraid of him.

More than that, she *couldn't* be afraid of him, she wasn't going to spend her days hiding in the palace, trying to avoid him. She was stronger than that.

She would be stronger than that.

"Why is that?"

"I aim to have the wedding take place quickly, and

a celebration so soon after the sheikh's death would be distasteful."

"Well, I can't say I'm too sad to avoid the big wedding."

"Neither can I." Though she would be happier to avoid a wedding altogether.

"You have not touched your dinner."

"I don't think I'll be hungry for a week at least."

"You have to eat. You'll get too thin."

She looked down at her increased figure and back up at him. "Losing baby weight wouldn't hurt my feelings."

"You don't need to lose any weight."

She looked up at him and realized that his eyes were focused on her breasts. She fought a surge of heat that bloomed at her midsection and spread outward. She should be offended. Instead, she was intrigued.

She couldn't remember having a man look at her breasts before. The men she interacted with were like her. Focused and driven, with tunnel vision when they were working on solving equations. Yes, there were obviously students and professors at the university who had relationships. Plenty of them. But while they were at school, they were at school.

And she chose to extend that kind of drive, focus and exclusion to the rest of her life. She'd never wanted a relationship and so had never really cared whether or not men looked at her breasts.

It was...interesting. And she really, really should be angry.

She cleared her throat but he didn't adjust the trajectory of his gaze. "Well, that's beside the point. The point is that in the space of a few days my life has changed completely."

Now he looked at her face. "Your life started changing nearly a year ago. And again when Aden was born. This is just an extension of that."

She bit the inside of her cheek. "I know."

It was true. Her life had been taken over when she'd gotten pregnant with Aden. The pregnancy had changed how she felt, how she looked, what she liked. Her body had been foreign to her, a stranger. Naively, she'd held on to the belief that after giving birth everything would be the same again.

She'd been so stupid.

"I'll never know how it would have been if they were still here," she said, her tone soft. "Would it have been easier to give him up?"

He shrugged. "Likely. You were confident that they would do a good job raising him."

She nodded. "I was."

"And are you confident that I would?"

"Not in the least," she said, not seeing the point in lying.

He didn't miss a beat. "Then I'm certain had Rashid and Tamara lived, you would have been fine."

She wasn't sure, though. Wasn't sure if she ever

really could have dealt with this the way she imagined she could.

"Probably."

"It does no good to castigate yourself for things that will never happen."

"I suppose you're right."

"Naturally," he said.

"You're so arrogant."

He shrugged. "As are you in the right setting. You have complete confidence in your abilities as a scientist, in your thought process and problem solving skills, I imagine."

"Of course I do."

"Then I fail to see why I should have anything less than complete confidence in my own domain."

"It's because it seems nothing falls outside of your domain," she said drily.

"I already told you I'm sure you could outtalk me on string theory."

"Then I'll stay in my science corner where I reign supreme." The words gave her some comfort. It really might not be so bad being married to him. She could spend time with Aden and spend time in that gorgeous study he'd had put together for her.

"You are welcome to your corner."

"Ah, generous," she said, looking down at her food and thinking that now she might chance a bite. And then she remembered how he'd looked at her breasts. Why had he been looking at her breasts?

She took a bite of rice and chewed while she pondered this new mystery of the universe. She could feel his eyes on her again and heat crept over her skin.

"I am not master of every domain, *habibti*," he said, his voice quiet. "You need only to look at the headlines to realize that."

"That's just public perception. It's not necessarily reality."

"There was an event, shortly after Rashid died, and a diplomat from a neighboring country wanted to speak to me about an upcoming rugby match between our two countries."

"And?"

"And I told him, quite succinctly, that I didn't care about sport at the moment, all things considered. He was unhappy, said he would not be encouraging his people to patronize Attar when they were to go on holiday. My response was to tell him to go to hell."

"Oh."

"That made for very salacious news, I can tell you. The next time we had an event at the palace, my advisor told me to be nice. Like I was a child." He laughed, the sound carrying no humor. "No, I am not the master of every domain."

"Well," she said, "I'm not either. And, strangely, I even work at proving myself wrong a lot of the time. It's what a good scientist does. Searches objectively for truth, regardless of their own personal beliefs. I guess a good leader has to be nice to everyone regardless of their own personal mood."

"I'm not sure I know how to be nice."

She looked at him, at his coal-dark eyes. "You aren't that bad, Sayid."

"Tell me, Chloe, what were you going to do before all of this?"

She was surprised by the question, even more surprised by the genuine curiosity behind it. "I was also due to start student teaching in the fall. And I'm gearing up to write my doctoral dissertation on how matter and energy behave on the molecular scale." Unlike having her figure stared at, in this, she had some confidence, total understanding. "After that, I had hoped to get a position at a research lab, and then a university as soon as I could manage it."

"You seem to enjoy doing paperwork." He said the word as though it was a scourge.

"I love it. But then, I think being a scientist is committing yourself to studying for the rest of your life. And I love that. I always want to learn and grow. I want to find out how it all works."

"Being a scientist takes a lot of curiosity," he said, his eyes dropping to her lips. And just like that, the air between them thickened, tightened. Her breasts felt heavy, her entire body languid and restless at the same time, which was simply an impossibility, and yet beneath his dark gaze, it was. "Do you consider yourself curious, Chloe?"

She cleared her throat. "I suppose so." Their eyes met and held, and she felt something tighten inside of her, her breath catching. "Are you...curious, Sayid?"

She'd known, before she'd spoken, that the words would be layered with double entendre, and yet she'd still spoken them. But the minute she did, she knew it was a mistake. Knew she'd crossed into a zone that was way, way out of her league.

Heat flickered in his dark gaze and she could feel inside of her, burning her. "About certain things," he said, his voice low. Husky.

She stood up quickly, her chair tilting slightly and knocking into the chair next to it, the sound loud in the cavernous room. "Sorry, sorry." She tried to straighten them, her cheeks burning, her heart pounding. "I have to go."

Sayid was faster than she was, his movements smoother. He crossed to her side of the table and caught her arm, drawing her to him, his expression dark. "Why are you running from me?"

"I'm not," she said, her voice a choked whisper. "I'm full."

"You hardly touched your dinner," he said, reaching up with his other hand to push a strand of hair out of her face.

"I'm not that hungry. Stress and all. You know, interesting thing about stress it can actually clog your pores and create—"

"I'm not interested in the side effects of stress," he said, his tone heavy, rough.

"Well…I'm just…explaining."

"Why are you running from me?" he asked again,

dipping his face lower, his expression fierce. "It's because you know, isn't it? You feel it?"

"Feel what?" she asked.

"This…need between us. How everything in me is demanding that I reach out and pull you hard against me. And how everything in you is begging me to."

"I don't know what you're talking about," she said.

"I think you do." He lowered his hand and traced her collarbone with his fingertip, sliding it slowly up the side of her neck, along her jawbone.

She shook her head, pulling away from him, from his touch. "No," she lied, "I don't."

She didn't understand what was happening with her body, why it was betraying her like this. She'd never felt this kind of wild, overpowering attraction for anyone in her life. But if she was going to, it would have been for a nice scientist who had a large collection of dry erase pens and looked good in a lab coat.

It would not be for this rough, uncivilized man who believed he could move people around at his whim. This man who sought to control everything and everyone around him.

Unfortunately, her body hadn't asked her opinion on who she should find attractive. Because that was most definitely what this was. Scientific, irrefutable evidence of arousal. Increased heart rate, swollen lips, tightening nipples, oh…dear…and yes, wetness between her thighs.

But if there was one thing she knew about attraction it was that it was physical, and she was not a physical creature. Her body was nothing more than a slave to its base, biological urges, but she was a woman who used her mind. A woman who reasoned and made choices based on things that had nothing to do with being in close proximity to a man with high testosterone.

"We may not have to play like this is a love match, but we will show my country that the marriage is real enough and that means you can't get up and run away during dinner parties."

"I wasn't running away," she bit out.

He slid his thumb over the exposed skin on her arm. "I don't believe you."

"It doesn't matter what you choose to believe or not. I was just ready to go back to my room. And study. Molecules."

"Then stay," he said, a challenge laced in his words. "Stay and talk to me."

The way he said "talk," didn't sound as if he wanted to talk at all. She had no experience with situations like this. Had never had the inclination to cultivate any. Now she sort of wished she had some, wished there was some way she could play cool and sophisticated.

But there was simply no way. Not only did she lack experience, but him being so dominant and so very, very male was off-putting to her. Which is what made it all so strange. Because the very things about him that scared her the most were also the things that she seemed to find most attractive.

More compelling evidence as to why her body should not call the shots.

"Fine," she said. "But I might have an easier time thinking of what to say if you let go of my arm instead of manhandling me like *Ardipithecus ramidus*." She couldn't help but chuckle at her own joke.

"What?"

"*Ardipithecus*…oh, come on. It's funny. It's one of the evolutionary stages of man. No? Nothing?"

"I assume you're calling me a Neanderthal."

"Well, sure if you want to oversimplify it."

He released his hold on her. "You're implying that I'm uncivilized, and make no mistake, Chloe, it's very true. I don't pretend to be otherwise."

"I've noticed."

"No matter how we feel about each other you and I will have to learn to get along in public, at the very least. We can hardly go to public functions only to end up sniping at each other."

"True, yeah, you have a point there."

"And you should refrain from implying that any important heads of State are more closely related to monkeys than men."

"Says the man who told a diplomat to go to hell." He treated her to a hard look. "Fine. I promise to reserve those insults for you, and even then, only in private."

It was strange, because just a few moments ago

she'd been thinking about how off-putting she found his masculinity, and yet, now, she was talking to him as though nothing had happened. She'd assumed his being so masculine had bothered her because the strength of men, especially men with power, was something she'd learned to fear.

But no matter how many times she struck out at Sayid verbally, and even the time she'd done so physically, he'd never made a move to hurt her in any way.

She was confident now that he wouldn't. So what was it that frightened her? Because she was frightened, no question about that.

"Careful, when you say things like that, it sounds a bit like an invitation that I don't think you're making," he said.

And then she realized just what scared her so much. The attraction and the fear were one. For the first time in her life, she was curious about sex in a way that went beyond the intellectual.

She didn't like it. Not one bit, particularly given the situation and the man who was piquing the curiosity. Detachment was important. It was her protection.

"You're right about that. I'm not making an invitation," she bit out, backing away from him. More because of herself than him. Because for a moment part of her had considered telling him that she was issuing an invitation. And then she wanted to sit back and see what he would make of that, because she didn't know what move she would make after that. She didn't know enough about the whole sex thing to make the next move.

Not like she didn't know how sex worked, just that she had no idea how one went about instigating it, particularly with a man like Sayid who had very clearly been there and done that.

It didn't bear thinking about at all, because she was not going to go near him. Not in that way. Not ever.

"And I would decline if you were."

The statement hit her right in the feminine ego. Not that she should be surprised by it. Men like Sayid hardly went for slightly chubby gingers who preferred Bunsen burners to boys and who had never even engaged in a good make out session.

"Well…moot. Because I already said I'm not inviting. Nope."

"Good," he snapped. Clipped. Hard.

Her cheeks heated, mortification washing over her, and it just served to make her even more angry. She shouldn't care that he didn't want to have sex with her, she didn't want to have sex with him! Well, she *wouldn't* have sex with him.

Maybe she sort of wanted to kiss him. At least, she wondered what it would be like to press her mouth to those hard, sculpted lips. To run her fingertip along the line of his jaw.

But that was all. Just idle wondering about a little kiss. Which was completely understandable. And normal. Lots of women probably thought about kissing him. And that, again, came back to biology because it certainly wasn't his sparkling personality.

"Fine. Well, I'm leaving now. Not running, mind you. Especially since we established that you aren't after my body."

"Have a good evening," he said, lips tight.

"Sure," she tossed back, turning and stalking out of the room.

As soon as she got into the corridor, she stopped and leaned against the wall, hand on her chest, trying to still the beating of her heart. She closed her eyes and breathed slowly, in and out. She felt dizzy.

She had to get a handle on this. And she would. The physical had never mattered to her, and it wouldn't start mattering now.

It couldn't.

Sayid needed a cold shower. But he had a call to make first. He paced the length of his office and punched in the speed dial for Alik Vasin.

"Da?"

"Vasin?" Sayid knew his friend's voice, but wanted to get confirmation anyway. A formality that was necessary when a man did the sort of work Alik did. Or at least, had done. He knew the ex-mercenary wasn't for hire anymore, not in that capacity. At least, not officially.

Sayid had hired him for his last job of that kind, and an unlikely bond had grown from there. Especially since Alik had been the one to spearhead the mission to get Sayid out of the enemy camp. Since Alik had been the one to find him, to keep looking when everyone else had given up.

"Da." There was music in the background, a woman speaking a language Sayid couldn't place, and then the sound of a door closing and the noise ending.

"Thank you for finding him."

"It is nothing. Easy."

"For you." Alik was Sayid's closest friend. A brother in many ways, more than Rashid had been even.

"For anyone. She was practically in the phone book."

"She wants to stay."

"With the boy?"

"Yes."

Alik let out a short grunt that could have meant approval, disapproval or something completely neutral. "I didn't figure she would want to stay because of you. And what did you tell her?"

"If I am to keep Rashid's secret, having her here could be problematic."

"Yeah, it could be." There was a pause. "You are avoiding my question which only piques my curiosity. What did you tell her?"

"I asked her to be my wife."

His friend laughed, genuine, filled with humor. He wasn't sure how Alik did it. How he had lived through all of the things he had, seen and done the things he'd seen and done, and emerged with a smile. Alik lived fast and hard. Honor falling far behind pleasure on his list of important things in life.

Sayid envied him sometimes. Envied the ease with which the other man lived. That he was able to somehow be invincible, and a man, at the same time.

"That's a bad idea, *comrade*. There is nothing worse than a wife."

"Have you ever had one?"

"No. And not by accident."

"Then how do you know?"

"I know because there is a blonde in my room tonight, and last weekend there was a brunette. Tomorrow, who knows? You cannot have that if you're married."

"Some men do."

"Then what is the point of making vows? I never made a vow I didn't keep."

"You don't make many vows."

Alik laughed again. "No. No, I don't."

"You made one to me."

"I did. And I did not make it lightly. You have my loyalty. Whatever you need, consider it done."

"And you have mine. There will be a wedding. A small one, out of observance for Rashid's death."

"You need security," Alik said.

"Naturally."

"You want me."

"Of course."

"Is this your version of asking me to be best man?"

The corners of Sayid's mouth twitched, the closest thing to a real smile he'd managed in too many years to count. "Best man with a handgun."

Sayid heard a door open on the other end of the line, the music, the woman, again. Then finally, Alik responded. "I'll do it."

For the second time in her life, Chloe watched her life change through a news story. It was all over the TV. An announcement that interim ruler of Attar, Sheikh Sayid al Kadar, was taking a wife. The hero nanny who had disregarded her own safety to protect the miracle prince.

She felt her jaw go slack as the story played across the screen. As a picture of her flashed onto it. Then a picture of Sayid. She cringed at the sight of herself, squeezed into the only dress she had. She still wasn't used to her fuller figure, and she could hardly call herself a fan of the look.

The female anchor was making eye contract with the camera, and talking about Chloe. A surreal experience for sure. "The stoic regent of Attar has announced his engagement to the heroine of the people, Chloe James, a part-time nanny and science student from Portland, Oregon. The wedding will be a small affair, appropriate for a nation still in mourning, and will take place a week from Saturday."

"Ugh." She groaned and turned the TV off, then turned around to face her whiteboard again. She'd been working an equation as part of her course work for half the morning while Aden lay on a blanket on the floor, kicking his feet in a slow, jerky fashion.

She leaned in and put her pen on the surface, trying to wipe the images on the screen from her mind, which was completely impossible to do. Completely.

She looked back at Aden, tugging her glasses off. "What am I getting myself into?" she asked. She got nothing from him, his blue eyes scanning the room, his fist finding his mouth.

Chloe blew out a breath. "No advice?"

"Why exactly do you need advice?"

She turned and saw Sayid striding toward her with purpose and that maddening self-assurance of his.

"I just saw my engagement announcement on the news," she said. "Along with the information that our wedding is less than a week away. Imagine my surprise."

"Why wait?"

"I don't know. There's no reason to, I suppose."

He shook his head once and reached into his pocket, producing a small box and holding it out to her. "I had my family's jeweler take a gem from the Crown Jewels and set it into a ring for you."

She flipped open the top of the box. "From the Crown Jewels?" She examined the piece. It was gorgeous, utterly perfect and unique.

A garnet, deep and clear, set into bright yellow gold, fashioned into vines that held the stone in place like a glittering flower.

"This is a little…much, don't you think?" she asked, touching the jewel with her fingertip. It struck her then, that no one had ever given her a gift. A strange realization, especially when this wasn't a gift, but a piece of the facade.

It felt like one, though. And not just any gift, something extravagant and beautiful. Something special. The sort of thing her parents never would have done for her because she was simply an after-thought.

It was embarrassing to realize how badly she wanted to put it on. How badly, in that moment, she wanted it to be special. How badly she wanted some-one, even if it was Sayid, to think she was special enough to deserve something so incredible.

She closed the lid on the box. On the feeling.

She didn't need that. Aden was her family. The only family she needed.

"Do you like it?" he asked.

"Of course. But I don't need a piece of the Crown Jewels."

"You do. Because every al Kadar woman is pre-sented with a piece of it for her wedding, and you will be no exception."

"It's not a real marriage."

"So give it back when we divorce."

She cleared her throat. "And when…when do you think that will be, exactly?"

"When will you be ready to live apart from Aden?"

She shook her head. "I won't. Not until he's grown."

"Then we will be married until then." He studied her closely. "It is a big commitment for someone your age. For someone whose life is outside of the royal family."

"Having a baby is always a big commitment. When a woman finds out she's pregnant…in that instant, her whole life changes. Her whole future changes. That's all that's happened to me. Yes, the circumstances are more complicated. And yes, the change happened a little later. But I'm willing to change my expectations of life for him. More than that, I want to."

"You will be a good mother for him," he said, his voice steady. Serious. "You will be the mother Tamara would have wanted for him."

Emotion swelled in her chest, and again she was conscious of the empty space in her that wanted so badly to be filled by another person. She wanted him to take her in his arms, to tell her everything would be fine. To simply hold her up for a while so that it wasn't only her strength keeping her from falling to her knees.

But she couldn't afford the weakness. Not when Aden needed her.

"Thank you," she said.

"Now, there is the small matter of lovers," he said, changing the subject with a shocking swiftness that made her head spin.

"Of what now?"

"Lovers," he said.

"I mean, I heard you, I just wasn't sure what you… meant…by it?"

"If I am not in your bed, I will, at some point during our marriage, be in the bed of another woman. I am willing to give up a lot for my country, and to give Aden the best life he can have, but I am not giving up sex for sixteen years."

She blinked. She supposed asking that of him was completely unreasonable. And yet, there was a small spark of anger, jealousy, inside that started in her stomach and flared up to her chest, making her heart pound hard.

Not so much jealousy in a possessive way. Not because she couldn't bear the thought of sharing him, which would be silly, all things considered. But because a part of her very much wanted to be the woman in his bed. Wanted to be the one he couldn't abstain from and, more than anything, be the one to benefit from his experience.

So stupid, Chloe.

The idea of seeing him with other women, of watching them parade through the palace in…tiny nighties with their big fake boobs bobbing up above the necklines for all the staff to see, made her stomach clench tight.

"Just…whatever you do," she said, "be discreet. I don't want to be conscious of what's going on inside your bedroom. You keep it in there, I won't open the door. To you, you can be getting some, to me, you can be in there all by yourself. And unless I open the door you can be both promiscuous and celibate. It'll be Schrodinger's affair."

"Because it's impossible to prove unless the door is opened?"

"Yeah, exactly. That's the joke."

"You need to work at cultivating more mainstream humor."

"That would have killed in Advanced Quantum Field Theory."

"The same applies to you. When you take a lover, you must use complete discretion. There can be no hint of a scandal for the media. None at all."

"Um…okay." She was celibate no matter which side of the door you stood on, and she had been for all of her life, so the idea of taking a lover after her marriage, after becoming a mother, seemed a little out there for her.

But she wasn't going to admit that, either. The only thing worse than knowing Sayid was getting action with some gorgeous girl, was knowing that she wasn't getting any action with an equally gorgeous guy. Which had never, ever mattered to her before. Stupid that it seemed to now.

"This is very serious, *habibti*. If I get caught in a scandal, very few people will care. I am a man in a man's world, and when it comes to sex, men are forgiven much. Women are not. If anything happens there will be an outcry for me to divorce you. This marriage is about image, and nothing must compromise that. Nothing can be done to damage the way the people see you."

"Don't worry. I will be the soul of discretion when engaging in my illicit affairs. No sex on the dining table," she said, and she felt her cheeks heat. She was trying to play at being sophisticated and worldly, trying to pretend she could stand there discussing just how their extramarital affairs would work without feeling horrifically awkward and embarrassed. It wasn't working.

His eyes darkened, his jaw tightening. "On the dining table? I think that would be quite uncomfortable anyway."

She swallowed. "Shows how much you know."

"I could show you how much I know."

The words escaped Sayid's lips without his permission. He should not press this. Should not push her to see how far the attraction could take them. But it was so easy to embrace, the images flashing through his mind, hot and fast.

As hard surfaces went, the dining table didn't feature in his fantasies. But against the wall? Her legs wrapped around his waist? That he could most certainly work with.

He could strip her of her clothes, of every inhibition. Could knock every fact she knew about the universe out of her head while she cried out her pleasure. And he would take his own in her gladly.

He clenched his teeth, tightening his hands into fists, trying to ignore the raging of his heart, the rush of blood south of his belt. He couldn't afford to burn off his sexual frustration with Chloe. Couldn't afford to let passion of any kind erupt between them.

Control was essential, keeping his defenses up, was essential. Always. And most especially with her. Why, he wasn't certain, but he knew that it was. Sex, the desire for it, for a woman, should not make him shake inside. And yet she did.

Which was why he could never touch her.

"I...that's okay. I don't need you to." Thankfully, Chloe was as wary as he should be. She bent down and scooped Aden into her arms, holding him tight against her chest, using him as a shield.

"As you wish."

"And I do. Wish it. That way."

"I have business to take care of before the wedding. I'll meet you at the coastal palace."

"Is that where the wedding will be?"

"Yes. A small ceremony on the beach."

"You have all of this figured out, don't you?"

He chuckled, no humor behind the sound. There never was with him. No happiness. No lightness. And it made her heart burn. "At this point, there is very little I would claim to have figured out, Chloe James."

CHAPTER EIGHT

THE OCEAN SIDE PALACE was an entirely different world to the main palace in central Attar. Here everything was washed white by the sun. The salt breeze coming in from the waves cooled the air, infused it with moisture, so unlike the arid heat found inland.

Sayid had spent a great deal of time at this palace growing up. A retreat from the times spent in the desert, living in Bedouin tents and learning how to survive in the harshest of environments.

Even now, walking into the cool, white stone foyer lifted a weight from him.

And then the realization that he was getting married in less than twenty-four hours, on the beach in front of the palace, hit him full force and any sense of Zen was lost entirely.

A wife. He had long given up the thought of having a wife. Thinking of marriage made him think of a different time. Of a beautiful girl with liquid brown eyes and a bright smile. Of the same girl, pale and terrified as she was forced into a car, taken from her home. Taken from him.

As he stood, men holding him in place, preventing him from going after her. Keeping him from rescuing her. From saving the only person who had ever mattered.

He put his hand on one of the white stone pillars, relished the chill that seeped through his skin. He looked out at the ocean, crashing into the rough, imposing rocks that stood sentry in front of the palace. He moved his palm over the pillar, so cold, like everything inside of him. As it had been since the day he'd lost Sura.

"She's upstairs, on the balcony. Getting her henna done." Alik was standing at the foot of the staircase, his hands in the pockets of his dark slacks.

"How long have you been here?" Sayid asked.

He and Alik had been through hell and back together. He was Sayid's only friend. The only person who understood what the kind of life he led was like. What it cost. But at the moment, happiness wasn't his dominant emotion when he looked at the other man. It was something else. Something dark, visceral and unfamiliar.

"Long enough to have bent her over the dining table out on the balcony once, taken her up against the wall in the bedroom twice, and in the bed..."

"Alik," he said, striding forward.

"In theory," Alik finished. "Every woman I desire is at my disposal, why would I touch yours?"

"She's not my woman," he said.

"She's going to be your wife by this time tomorrow."

"Only in name. Only on paper."

"Not in your bed? A waste of a beautiful woman."

Sayid strode past Alik and started up the curved, white stone staircase. "I don't require your opinion on the matter, Vasin."

Alik shrugged and walked to the bottom of the stairs. "I'll leave you to your fiancée. I have some security measures to check." Alik disappeared around the corner, and Sayid continued on up the stairs, anger still coursing through his veins. There was no reason for it, not really.

Had he not told Chloe he would be taking other lovers? And had he not extended the same courtesy to her? Neither of them were likely to be celibate for sixteen years, and if Alik was one of the lovers she chose, could he truly be territorial about it?

Yes, dammit.

There was a line. And Alik would not cross it. He would make sure the other man knew that.

Sayid stalked down the hall and toward the open doorway that led out to the balcony that overlooked the sea. He saw Chloe, sitting in a plush chair, wearing a very small dress. Aden was in a bassinet at her feet, and an elderly woman was kneeling in front of her, singing softly and painting intricate designs on Chloe's hands and feet.

Chloe looked up sharply, shimmering strands of red hair catching the light, the backdrop of the blue ocean highlighting the depth of her eyes. She had no makeup on, but then, Chloe rarely did. Nothing beyond the minimum. But something about her struck him as different. Fresh, her freckles clearly visible, her skin pink.

She was brighter, he realized. Not as exhausted. The dark circles under her eyes had faded away.

"I wasn't expecting you so soon," she said.

The woman who was working on the henna turned and bowed her head low, her forehead brushing the ground, then she turned back and continued on with her design. The display meant nothing to him. A customary show of servitude. But at this point, one he gladly took as a positive sign that he was being accepted in his temporary position. That his impending marriage to Chloe was having the desired effect.

"When were you expecting me to show up? Just in time for vows?"

"Something like that," she said.

"Well, I'm not quite so last-minute. I wanted to go over security measures with Alik."

"Oh, right."

He watched her face closely when he said his friend's name. "You've met Alik?"

"Of course. He's very friendly."

"How friendly exactly?" he asked, his teeth gritted.

"Well he…" She cut herself off. "Are you…irritated?"

"No."

"You are. Are you…bothered by the fact that he was friendly to me?"

He snorted. "That's ridiculous. I would hope he was friendly to you. You are the future sheikha of Attar."

She tilted her head to the side and squinted, as if she was studying a specimen beneath a microscope. "You…are you jealous?"

"I am not given to the emotion in any circumstance. Not even with a woman who is my lover. There is absolutely no reason I would feel it in connection with you."

"That's very true. There isn't a reason. Except that I'm marrying you tomorrow and while the institution is human in concept, the idea of a male possessing his mate with some form of exclusivity runs across species. How else can a male be certain his offspring is truly his?"

"The offspring in this instance is not mine, as you well know. And as I don't—" he looked down at the woman, still working on Chloe's feet "—as you are well aware, our situation is different."

"But it's a deep-seated male need, so the fact that your brain knows it doesn't necessarily mean your body does."

He arched one brow and looked at her. Color crept into her cheeks slowly, staining the freckles a darker shade. "I suppose that is true," he said, just for a moment, one moment, embracing the dark, restless ache that spread through his body whenever he looked at her. Acknowledging what it was. Attraction. Lust. Letting himself fully visualize all the fantasies that had been rioting through his brain in fuzzy, half-formed pictures for over a week.

Her body, beneath his, arching into him as he chased his release inside of her. Bending her over, making her grip the headboard, hands tight on her hips as he thrust inside.

Oh, yes, that was what he wanted.

And he would not allow himself to have it. Because the lust he felt for her wasn't simple. It went deeper, went to a place he had to deny existed. The place with all the cracks. The place that held his weakness.

"You think you know what it is my body wants?" he asked, aware that his voice sounded rough.

The color in her cheeks deepened. "I mean, in terms of…the fidelity aspect and the um…reproductive um…and laying claims to offspring, and so on…well…yes?"

He chuckled, letting the erotic images of a few moments before replay in his mind. "No. I don't think you know what my body wants. I'm not sure you know what yours wants, either."

She frowned, lush lips pulled down. "That's ridiculous. Of course I know what my body wants."

"But you think I don't?"

"No, I think what your body wants and what your mind believes to be true are at odds. That's different."

"I see. And what is it your body wants, Chloe?"

He waited, watched as she seemed to have a mini-realization. Her lips parted slightly, her eyes widening. "Not…not that," she said.

It was as though she'd only just picked up on the depth of the innuendo in the conversation. And that seemed strange to him. A woman of her age and beauty, should be well aware of the undertones to conversations between men and women. She should be well versed in the words beneath the words.

Yet, it seemed as though she wasn't. He wasn't sure how that could be possible.

"Alik is off-limits," he said, deciding that the direct approach would work best with her.

She wrinkled her nose. "You're telling me this because you honestly thought I would… Ugh."

He looked down at the woman kneeling before Chloe. She was putting the finishing touches on the flower, and as soon as she had completed the task, he spoke to her in Arabic. "You are dismissed."

She nodded once and gathered her things, walking quickly from the deck without looking at either Chloe or him.

"What did you say to her?" Chloe asked.

"I told her she could go."

"She didn't look at us."

"Giving us our due respect."

"I don't require that people treat me like…like that."

He shrugged. "I don't require it. But I gladly accept it. It's a sign that no one is out to oppose me. There are reasons that deference is appreciated. Especially given how well received I was initially."

"Hmm," she said, crossing her arms beneath her breasts, her eyes trained on the vines that curled around her foot and back behind her ankle.

"You disapprove?"

"Does it matter?"

"No. But I am curious."

"Fine. It's just another way that patriarchal men reinforce their dominance. I grant you, it's not the most despicable way, but it's a way."

"There are plenty of queens in the world, *habibti*. Queens who are intent on crushing their subordinates beneath a spiky heel. Don't think it is unique to men."

"Well, you're not making a great case for it in terms of behavior." She stood, swooping down to collect Aden. He noticed that she was more confident now with the baby than when he'd first met her. "Coming out here playing the part of territorial wolf. Trying your best to claim exclusive rights on a, uh…a caribou carcass you don't even want."

"Did you just compare yourself to a caribou carcass?"

"Unfortunate parallel aside," she said, "the point remains valid."

"I never said I didn't want you," he said. The words torn from him, the admission unwelcome. And they hung between them, thickening the tension that had building ever since the first moment he'd seen her.

He took a step toward her, her scent, sweet, feminine, filled with honeysuckle, grabbed his throat and threatened to choke him with his lust.

She was very wrong if she thought he didn't know what he wanted. He knew. And it involved her naked and crying out his name, with pleasure rather than the complete frustration he usually heard coming from her.

"But I...you. You did. I'm sure you did. There was all kinds of talk about other lovers and...and I'm sure the implication was..."

"That I'm not committing myself to a sixteen-year exclusive relationship with you. Which means it's best if nothing ever happens between the two of us."

"Oh. But...but it could. You're saying it could in terms of...because you're...are you attracted to me?"

The way she asked the question, the utter lack of guile and calculation in the words, was astonishing to him. It was as if she'd missed the tension. No, she hadn't, he was sure of that, but it was as if she'd imagined she'd been the only one to feel the electricity arching between them.

Everything in him wanted to wrap his arm around her waist and pull her to him, to show her, exactly, how he felt. To press his lips to the hollow of her throat, lick the indent at her collarbone. Continue down to the valley between her breasts.

But she was holding the baby like a very convenient, living shield.

"Am I attracted to you?" he asked, taking another step toward her, desire flooding through him, hot, reckless. "When I arrived here and saw Alik, and I thought there was a chance he might make a play for you, I had fantasies of tying a rock around his neck and throwing him into the sea."

Chloe looked at Sayid, into the dark, intense eyes that were so sharply focused on her that she felt as if she'd been put beneath a microscope and cut open, so that every piece of her, every secret hidden from the naked eye, was on perfect display, out in the open for him and for anyone else to look at.

His voice was low, shaking with intensity. She wrapped her arms more tightly around Aden, her heart thundering heavily, her hands shaking. And for the first time she identified the tightening in her stomach, the racing of her pulse, with ease.

She was attracted to him. She desired him.

That had never happened to her before and it was making her feel a little dizzy.

"Then I came out here," he continued, moving to the side, circling her, slowly, like a predator who had spotted prey. "And my fantasies changed. I would have you," he said, his voice almost a growl. "Bent over in front of me. Saying my name as I brought you to pleasure, over and over again."

The pictures his words painted were so vivid, so shocking, the reaction they created so visceral, that she had to look away from him. Her face was burning, her breathing short, fast.

She knew how he would be, she didn't need experience to understand. He wanted to dominate her. To use her body against her. To create a kind of sexual euphoria that would put her under his spell.

No, she didn't think he would use violence against her. But Sayid had other power. And she knew he would use that.

And she had seen all that a woman would endure for the man who owned her body.

She wouldn't allow him to do that to her. Ever.

She moved away from him, trying to get her breathing under control. "As charming as that little bit of verbal pornography was, I'm going to have to say no."

"You aren't attracted to me?" he asked.

She could never lie all that convincingly, but who needed a lie when a well-placed insult would do? "I'm not impressed by your neanderthal behavior," she spat. "I'm not into the dominant male thing."

"Really?"

"Really. I agreed to this for Aden, but I didn't agree to this," she said, waving her hand in the space between them, "so if you're having a bout of pent-up sexual frustration, I suggest you go and find a willing woman to work it off with."

"That's what you want?" he asked, his voice taking on a deadly edge now.

"Yes," she lied, "it's what I want."

"I thought you wanted discretion?"

"Bend *her* over the balcony for all I care," she said, letting anger fuel her now, anger and fear, "it won't bother me."

She turned and walked back into the palace, fighting against the tears that were threatening to fall. She sat down on the lavish, four-poster bed that had been provided for her in her room and unbuttoned her shirt with one hand, unclipping her nursing bra and guiding Aden to her breast. She was getting used to this. To this part of motherhood. But Sayid…

She'd never been so confused, so afraid of her own body, in her entire life.

And the man who was causing her all this grief was the man she was marrying tomorrow.

There were few guests at the beachside wedding, and none of the usual Attari pre-ceremony traditions were being observed. No three-day feasts, no group dances and the henna party had, blessedly, only included one woman.

Chloe was thankful for those small favors, but she was still nervous about the event itself. Especially after her last encounter with Sayid. And, of course, she hadn't even bumped into him in the hall since she'd stormed away the evening before, all but commanding he find some other woman to do it with on their wedding night.

Not that it was their wedding night in any way that mattered.

It wasn't a wedding that mattered. The most important guests in attendance were a few carefully selected members of the press who would write up a nice story about the event and bestow hope upon a nation. In theory. Theirs had to be the most magical lie in history, if it really possessed all that power. But if it did, and the outcome was as good as predicted, she could hardly feel bitter about it.

As it was, for the moment, she felt a little bitter.

Think of Aden. And not of everything you're leaving behind.

She pressed her hands over her eyes and tried to breathe. It felt as though the sand was sliding beneath her feet, slipping away. Leaving her with nothing to stand on.

She heard the music change, heard her cue to walk down the aisle.

She took a deep breath and stepped out from behind the tent that had been raised on the beach for the dinner that would follow the ceremony, lifting the hem of her dress so that she wouldn't stumble over the delicate fabric. It was completely plain, a flowing, cream summer dress that brushed over the sand as she walked. A white, silken scarf covered her hair, shielding her from the sun. She didn't hold any flowers. She didn't have an attendant to take them from her when she reached her groom. She had no one standing there with her.

Her only family was Aden. The reminder of why she was doing this.

Poles were raised along the aisle, white silks wrapped around them, draped between them, blowing in the wind. It was utter perfection in its simplicity, the waves on the shore the only music, with few decorations to mar the natural beauty of the sand and surf.

She raised her eyes and saw Sayid, standing at the head of the aisle, the wind blowing the silks, partially obscuring him from view. But for a moment, their eyes locked and held. Darkness, heat, crackled between them. She looked down. It was traditional for the bride to keep her eyes down anyway. To keep herself from smiling. To not appear too eager.

Which was good, because not-smiley and not-eager, were coming easily at the moment.

She kept going until she saw his shoes, half-buried by sand, come into her field of vision. Then she looked up. He was dressed like she was, simple, not entirely in the Attari tradition, but not entirely Western, either. His shirt was white, loose over his muscular frame, as were his slacks. His shoes were white as well, simple, embroidered with gold thread.

The strength of his masculine beauty, the impact that it had on her, was shocking. She would have thought that after yesterday, after those bold, awful, *yes* they were totally awful, things he'd said to her, she would despise the sight of him. But she didn't.

And part of her didn't think the things he'd said had been so awful, either.

Part of her had been intrigued. And wanted to

hear more. Had wanted him to show her just what he'd meant.

It was so not the time to be having those thoughts. Though, there would never be a good time for those thoughts. Ever.

Sayid stood facing her, but not touching her, the distance between them welcome.

The ceremony started in Arabic and Sayid leaned in, her heart stalling out as he drew near to her. Then he began to translate softly, the words husky, smooth. So unlike the way he'd spoken to her yesterday. And no less impacting. These were words of commitment, of caring not of lust or domination. About the meaning of marriage, the soul deep bond of it. A meaning she had never before witnessed, but that something deep within her ached to have.

When it came time for her to say her vows, she repeated them as best she could, with no idea of what she was promising to do before the officiant and all of the witnesses. She knew her Arabic was clumsy and very likely completely unintelligible, and she just hoped that the headline tomorrow wasn't about the new sheikha who had garbled her vows.

As soon as she spoke the last word, she nearly sagged with relief.

But then it was Sayid's turn to take his vows. And he chose to repeat them in English.

"I will not leave you, or turn back from you," he said, his voice strong, his focus somewhere behind her. And for that she was grateful, because she was certain that eye contact was beyond her at this point. He still didn't touch her, didn't reach for her hand. "Where you make your home, I shall make mine. For without you there is no home. Your people are now my people, as mine are yours. Where you die I will die. And there they will bury me. May God deal with me severely if anything but death separates us."

Chloe tried to breathe, the sea air suddenly too harsh, too salty. Her chest ached, ached with a need so fierce she feared it would choke her.

She wished the vows had stayed a mystery. Wished she had never heard the promises they'd made to each other in a way she could understand. Because when they'd been foreign, it hadn't felt real. Hadn't truly felt like vows.

Now, though, now she felt the weight of them. It was as if an invisible thread had been wound around them, binding them together. As if they were linked now, in a way that was completely beyond reason or logic.

And as the bond tightened between them, she felt the ties to her old life being cut away, until all that remained was this. Was Attar, and Aden and Sayid. The weight of it, the sadness, the certainty in it, was almost enough to bring her to her knees.

None of this is real. She tried to remind herself, tried to shift her focus back to the reasons behind the wedding. The practicality of it. Tried to stop the vows from echoing in her mind.

The officiant picked a bowl up from a small table

that was between Chloe and Sayid. It was filled with honey. He began to speak, loudly and for the guests, while Sayid translated for her ears only. "It is an Attari tradition, for the bride and groom's first taste of marriage to be sweet, that our life may always be sweet." He took her hand in his, and dipped her pinkie finger into the honey, then lifted it to his lips, closing his mouth around it, sucking the honey from her skin.

His lips were hot, his tongue slick. The intimate touch sent a shiver through her body. Violent. Unsettling. It left her shaking, aching.

He lowered her hand, then repeated the action with his own finger, extending it to her, touching his fingertip to her lips, requesting entry. She complied, opening her mouth for him.

The sweetness of the honey burst over her tongue first, warm and sticky, a shot of pure sugar. Then it faded, dissolving, giving way to the salt of Sayid's skin. Without thinking, she slid the tip of her tongue up the side of his finger, taking a taste of him that wasn't covered up by anything. A pure shot of Sayid that was as intoxicating as any alcohol.

She was almost reluctant to release him, which was as strange as anything that had happened to her since she'd agreed to marry him.

And now they were married. There were cheers from the guests, and blinding flashes from the photographer. Aden was sleeping through it, cradled closely by one of his nannies in the front row.

And then Sayid took her hand, the gesture distant in its way, formal. The way he did it, his forearm pressed against hers, his fingers curved around her hand, spoke of tradition. And yet, her body didn't seem to have gotten the memo.

A shot of heat fired through her, a sort of bone-deep longing she could scarcely identify. The truth was, she didn't want to identify it, because she knew what it was.

Because she knew that, no matter how much she wanted to pretend she didn't like the things he'd said to her yesterday, no matter how much she wanted to deny that the taste of his skin had made her heart beat faster, had made her breasts ache, it didn't change the fact that she did.

Like any scientific discovery, once something was found, once a hypothesis was introduced, it was impossible to close the lid on it again. It was there. It could never not be there again.

And she was curious by nature. A requirement of her field. She had to know things, had to know not just how they worked but why, and when, and for how long.

But this couldn't be the same. She couldn't follow this problem to a solution. Because this wasn't something she could sit and figure out on her whiteboard. There was no logical equation to Sayid. No set pattern of steps to work with to answer the question of what it would be like to have his lips on hers, to feel all that raw male passion directed at her, poured onto her with no restraint, with no denial on either side.

No. There was no way to figure that out with a whiteboard and a pen.

And the other option was simply not open for consideration.

CHAPTER NINE

THE RECEPTION FEAST HAD been laid out in a lush, silk tent. Punched tin lanterns hung from the supports, casting stars onto a rug-covered floor. Low tables were situated inside with silk pillows placed around them for the guests to sit on. Every table was full. Servants from both palaces were in attendance, celebrating with their sheikh. Celebrating the future.

Every tribal elder in Attar was there, seated at the table heads, along with diplomats and serviceman. As low-key as the wedding had been, the reception was anything but. A party in the truest sense of the word. Too bad Chloe wasn't in a party mood.

She and Sayid were sitting at a table on a raised pedestal, making it so that all eyes could easily be on them. There was music, laughing, talking. And Chloe was afraid that her head might burst from tension. It might not have been so bad if the vows hadn't been playing on continual loop in her mind.

If anything but death separates us...

Except sixteen years and the coming-of-age of Aden was meant to separate then. And they were never intended to be joined, not truly. Not on the kind of deep, spiritual level spoken of during their wedding ceremony.

Sixteen years. Sixteen years with the man beside her. Sixteen years away from her home.

Except thinking of Portland, of the green, rain-drenched landscape, didn't fill her with any sort of longing. Didn't make her ache with a need to be there. She didn't even feel a connection anymore. But Attar wasn't her home, either.

So when her marriage to Sayid was over, when Aden was grown, where would her home be? She already knew she couldn't go back. Because going back would be living as if this, as if Aden, as if Sayid, had never happened. As if she could be happy with the things she'd wanted before.

She knew she couldn't be.

The truly frightening thought was, whether or not Attar would be home in the end. If Sayid would be home.

She looked at him out of the corner of her eye. He was so handsome, his posture rigid, black eyes fringed with dark lashes focused intently on their guests. His skin was smooth, bronzed perfection, his cheekbones prominent. His lips…curved. Sensuous. She knew they could be cruel, too, she'd been on the receiving end of harsh words and sneers. But she also knew, with a kind of intuition that was born into her, that they would also be soft for a lover. Giving. Demanding.

No. She couldn't think about him that way. That was just craziness. Illogical on every level.

But no matter how illogical, part of her wanted to draw closer to him. To see if he was as hot and hard as he appeared. To see if his lips tasted as sweet as honey.

She sucked in a sharp breath and looked back down at her empty plate. She hardly remembered eating the lamb and lentils, but clearly, she had.

The drumbeat increased, became louder, the dominant sound in the room now, and one of the tribal leaders seated at the head of one of the long tables stood, speaking loudly in Arabic, his voice carrying over the music.

Sayid leaned in, a translation just for her. "He is wishing us long life. Happiness. Many children."

Her stomach clenched in anxiety. "Not gonna happen."

"And he is bidding us a good night, as we go to make the marriage official."

"What does he mean by that?" she asked.

Sayid stood, extending his hand to her, and she grasped it, allowing him to help her up. He waved and began to walk through the tent, leading her.

"What did he mean by that?" she wondered aloud.

"The vows, the feast, are all a part of the sealing of the marriage. But the marriage is not truly valid until the groom has possessed the bride in the ultimate way," he said, his voice smooth, deep. His words, however vague, were completely provocative, and she was certain he knew it. Certain he knew the kind of images it brought to her mind. The kind of ache it brought to her body.

"What?" she asked.

They exited the tent and cheers erupted behind them. "They will continue the party long into the night," he said, ignoring her question.

"In the United States, the marriage is legal when both parties and the appropriate witnesses sign a marriage license. Are you telling me that in Attar we actually have to…"

"That is the custom," he spoke calmly.

"And you knew," she said. "You knew. You said we wouldn't…that you wouldn't…"

"You are being hysterical now," he said as they walked into the palace, his words echoing in the empty corridor.

"Where is everyone?" she asked, looking around the empty hall. The palace was always bustling, staff everywhere, but not now. Now it was silent.

"They are enjoying the party, and giving us time to enjoy our private party." He took a step toward her and she retreated, her back hitting the wall.

"You are not forcing a wedding night on me," she said.

"No," he bit out, advancing on her. "I'm not." He pressed his palm against the wall behind her head, leaning in. "Although, we both know I wouldn't have to force you to do anything. You want it."

"I don't," she spat.

"Liar," he said. "I know you feel it. I see it in the way you look at me. Wide, curious eyes. You're hungry. For me."

"And you are an egotistical jerk who thinks that women will want him just because he's a man and it's his due!"

"No, I'm simply a man who can see. And I can see that you feel the same way I do. That no matter how badly you want to deny it, you want me."

"No," she repeated, "I don't."

No one had ever accused Chloe of being stupid. She'd been called a great many things in her life, but never that. And she knew, before she issued the denial, that doing so would be a challenge. A challenge that Sayid wouldn't let go unanswered.

And so she had issued it. Because she wanted the consequences. Craved them. Hungered for them. He was right, she was hungry. For something she'd never tasted. Something she'd spent her life avoiding so that she would never learn to want it.

He lifted the hand that had been resting at his side and placed it on her hip, sliding his fingertips over the thin fabric of her dress, the heat seeping through, branding her, sending a streak of fire through her veins.

His dark eyes never left hers as he leaned in, letting his hand drift upward to her waist, his thumb just brushing the underside of her breast.

"Then walk away," he whispered, angling his

head, his lips nearly touching the tender skin of her neck. "Walk away from me now."

"I…I…"

He put his other hand on her waist, both thumbs running beneath her breasts. So close. So very close to her tight, aching nipples. Oh, how she wanted him to move his hands. Not away, but up. To cup her breasts, to give her the touch, the pressure she so desperately desired.

"You won't," he said, hot breath fanning over her skin. "You won't because you're as desperate as I am."

She tried to swallow, but couldn't, her heart thundering so fast she was afraid it would beat out of her chest.

"There is something I'm regretting," he said.

"What's that?" she asked.

"That the Attari wedding tradition does not require the bride and groom to kiss."

"I don't regret it," she said, knowing she was challenging him again. Knowing there would be consequences.

"You don't sound very convincing," he said.

"Because I'm lying," she said.

He chuckled and then she felt the hot press of his mouth on her neck. "I thought you might be." His fingertip traced a line from her shoulder, up her neck, and along her jaw, then around her lips. "Yes, I was certain you were."

He moved then, his lips brushing against hers. "Tell me you want this," he said, his voice rough.

He was going to make her ask. Was going to make her drop her defenses, lay her pride down. Was going to force her to be weak before him.

But she already was. Too weak to stop herself from complying.

"I want it."

That was all it took. His lips were hard on hers, his kiss devouring, insatiable, proving she wasn't the only hungry one.

She'd wondered about kissing. More than once she'd wondered if it would be wet, or warm. If it would be awkward. If having someone's tongue in your mouth would be more gross than sexy.

She had her answer now. Warm, wet in the best possible way, not awkward in the least and...his tongue swept against the seam of her lips, requesting entry, and she gave it. And sexy. The answer to the last question was: sexy.

She returned the kiss, fully aware that her movements weren't anywhere near as smooth as his. That when she slipped her tongue between his lips, it wasn't with the kind of practiced confidence he possessed. But his hands curved around her back, pulling her tightly against him, she didn't care. Not at all.

She slipped her arms around his neck, fingers curling into his hair, holding him tightly to her mouth as she continued to taste, and to be tasted. Being tasted was her favorite part, she was pretty sure.

Then he growled. A rough, masculine sound that radiated from his body and through hers. Her back connected to the wall again, hard and cold behind her, Sayid hard and hot in front of her. Pinning her. Trapping her. And she didn't care.

As long as he kept touching her, as long as he kept kissing her, he could do whatever he wanted. As long as she could have this feeling.

An alarm went off in the back of her mind, the sane, rational voice that had dominated for so many years screaming at her to listen to her last thought. And a memory intruded, one that she should never have let fade. One she should have kept closer.

Why do you stay with him, Mom?

Because as bad as he makes me feel sometimes... when he makes it feel good, he makes it feel like heaven.

No.

She broke the kiss, gasping for air, shoving at his chest, blinding panic moving through her, taking over the pleasure that had made her behave so foolishly. So much like her mother.

"Stop," she said, her chest rising and falling quickly, her voice shaking. She was going to cry. She could feel it in the sting of her eyes, the ache in her throat, the sick feeling in her stomach. She didn't want him to see her tears.

"What's wrong?"

"What's wrong?" she asked, choosing to embrace anger. Anger was so much better than weakness. So much better than acceptance. "You…you're trying to dominate me by making me feel good. Trying to exert power over me with sex, but it isn't going to work."

"Funny, I thought I was kissing you. I thought I even gave you the chance to leave."

"You said it, but you were holding me there. You know that."

"And you could have broken away, like you did just now. You know that. Don't change it to suit you just because you're having regrets."

"Hopefully that's our marriage confirmed then, because that was quite enough for me," she said, breezing past him and heading for the stairs.

"Oh, no, *habibti,* that is not how a marriage is confirmed here. It will not be official until I'm inside of you."

She whirled around, her heart beating erratically. "Don't say things like that to me."

"Why? Because it makes you want it?"

"Because it's disgusting," she hissed, a tear escaping now, sliding down her cheek. "You have all the power here, and I won't let you have this, too." She turned away from him and went up the stairs, stalking down the hall and to her room. It was empty. Aden had been moved to the nursery for the night.

And she couldn't go and get him. Not if she hoped to keep up the pretense of being a true wife to Sayid.

In reality, she wouldn't be able to sleep in her room, either. She sat in a chair in front of an ornate vanity.

She wouldn't sleep, then.

But she wasn't going to Sayid's room.

Sayid felt as if a rock had settled in his stomach. He didn't know what had prompted her reaction to him, but he knew it came from somewhere deep. A place she kept hidden from the world. A place that had been created by pain.

He knew it because he recognized it. In his case, the pain had been so great that every nerve ending had been killed and cauterized. Leaving him healed, but not feeling. Never again.

With Chloe…her wounds were raw. Not enough to stop the pain. Not for the first time, he was grateful that he'd been spared that. That his wounds had been too grave to heal right.

He stood in the corridor for a long time, weighing what he would do.

He would follow her. Because she was in pain. Because she was his wife. And because for the first time in a very long time, he felt the desire to do the right thing, not the right thing in terms of honor or the greater good, but the right thing for a person.

Sayid followed the path Chloe had taken and knocked on her bedroom door. He heard nothing and he realized that she might be afraid he was a palace employee.

"It's me," he said.

"Why?" she asked, her voice a long whine.

"Because we have to talk."

"Well, come in. You don't want anyone to catch you in the hall."

He pushed the door open and felt a strange tightening in his chest when he saw her there, sitting at the vanity, her knees pulled up to her chest, her white dress flowing out around her.

"What happened down there?"

"I told you," she said.

"You gave me that same line you've been giving me. It always turns in to what a neanderthal I am. To how I'm trying to dominate you. Let me tell you something, Chloe, if I were trying to dominate you, you would know it. There would be no mistaking it."

Her cheeks turned red. "It's just that…you could, Sayid. You have…so much power. I can't give you any more."

"Attraction," he said, not sure why he was doing this, reaching out, but knowing he had to now, "is two sided. And it means you have power over me, as well. The power to make me lose my mind, like I did a few moments ago."

"I didn't…I don't…"

He crossed the room and knelt before her, gripping her chin with his thumb and forefinger, tilting her face up to his. "You did."

"Sayid, I can't…."

He tilted his head up and caught her lips with his, the kiss quick, a demonstration of what she made him feel. When they parted, he was breathing hard, his heart beating fast. He couldn't remember a time before Chloe when a simple kiss had possessed so much power.

Sex had always been easy for him to get. Women liked the combination of looks and power he possessed, and that meant from the time he'd wanted sex he'd been getting it with ease. So that had meant that a kiss had never been anything more to him than a prelude to the act.

But he wanted to savor it with Chloe. To kiss her slowly, deeply. Until she relaxed into him. Until she begged for more.

The fantasy had changed. He *had* thought of dominating her. Of taking his pleasure in her. Those images were gone now. How could he think of such a thing when she was sitting here like this, so brittle he feared she would break if he handled her too roughly?

Tenderness invaded him, a feeling that was so foreign he might have been experiencing it for the first time. He didn't know it was possible for him to feel it, not anymore.

Sura was the only woman, the only person, to ever make him feel the emotion before. And not since. Never since. He waited for the reminder of the woman and child he'd lost to kill the feeling, to come to his aid and remind him of why this was impossible for a man like him. Why he must never let himself feel.

It didn't work. And it made him angry. "Look at me," he growled. She complied. "Why are you afraid of me?"

"I'm not," she said, her breasts pitching up sharply with her indrawn breath.

"You are."

"It's not you," she said, her voice a whisper. "It's men."

The admission hit him like a physical blow. "All men?"

"Certain types of men. Men with power. Men who like power."

"What man doesn't like power? The alternative is to be without, and I don't think that's anyone's preference."

"It's different," she said, "for some. There's liking…control, I guess, over your own life. And of course people like that. I like that. I liked it, I miss it sometimes."

"You feel like you don't have control now?"

"I don't have control. You and I both know that." He nodded once and she continued. "But then there's…there are men, Sayid, that love to dominate. Love to control. Love to have power and watch how they can use it to control other people. And there are people who let them. Because of…of passion. That's what I'm afraid of."

He knew all about people like that. There were people like that who ruled countries, countries he'd had to go to war with. And in the prisons…the prisons were run by men like that. Men who liked to watch others in pain. Who liked causing it. He'd spent a year in the hands of a madman like that.

And that she'd seen something of that in him...it made him ill. That she'd seen it at all made his vision red, a haze of violence making it hard to see.

"Who hurt you, Chloe?" He knew his desire for blood was audible in his tone, knew that he sounded as enraged as he felt. Good. Let her hear it. Let her know that if it were in his power, the man who dared put his hands on her would die with Sayid's fingers curled around his throat.

The anger was suffocating, uncontrollable, as foreign in many ways as the tender emotion from a moment ago.

Chloe blinked rapidly. "I...he never touched me. I always wondered why. But then, I think for both of them life was better if they just ignored me."

"Who?" he ground out.

"My parents. My father. He..." She took a breath. "One of my first memories is just this one little clip. There isn't even sound. I remember I couldn't get something out of the fridge on my own, so I must have been very small. I was looking for my mom, so that she could get me a snack. I walked into her room, just in time to see my father put his hands on both of her shoulders and shove her against the dresser. She hit her head on the corner and fell. That's all I remember. I have a hundred more memories like that. My mother being bruised, my father hitting her. Knocking her unconscious. And I have a hundred more memories of them kissing. Having sex against the hallway wall like I wasn't there to walk in on my way out of my room."

She let the breath out, a slow, shuddering sound. "I hated it. So much. I hated that he had that power over her. I hated that she let him have it. I hated their passion."

"Is that why you're a scientist?"

"There is passion in science, but there's an order to it. Science is about fact, at the very least, it's about the pursuit of fact. To discover what *is*. To understand the world, the universe. To know how it works."

"You hoped it would make you understand?"

"I hoped. But I don't. Not yet. Maybe never. No… never. I never will. There is no answer to that, there's no logic to it. It's emotion. And emotion is…"

"Beyond logic," he said. "On that we can agree."

"I've given everything up for Aden," she said, her voice softer now. "And that makes sense. He can't take care of himself and he…he needs me. But I don't know what made my mother give up her right to basic human decency to hold on to a monster."

"People don't make sense," he said. "You and I have seen that. We've seen the darkness that lives inside the human heart."

"Yes," she whispered. "That's it exactly. And now I see it everywhere."

He nodded. "There is wisdom in that."

"But?" she asked.

"But, that is not how I see it."

"How do you see it?"

"I do not speculate. I find out what is, and what isn't, and I act. I don't waste time on emotion, or on worrying about that darkness. Rather, when I see it, I eradicate it."

"Do you know how much I wished I could?" she asked. "Sometimes...I wished I was strong enough to make him stop. I thought about it. Fantasized about it. And then one day I asked her why she didn't leave. She said the pleasure he gave her was worth the pain. And I realized she didn't want him gone. Or at least, she didn't think she did."

"Are they still together?"

She nodded. "But I don't go home. Ever. It was like being in prison. I won't ever go back."

"No. You would never choose to go back to something like that," he said.

He knew what a hell it was to watch others be tortured. He'd experienced it during his year in prison. It was why he never screamed. Although, he'd learned not to years before that. Pain had been inflicted on him early and often, an attempt to teach him to never break under threat of pain.

It was the one time he'd broken since Sura. And again, it had caused terrible devastation. He had deviated from the plan to prevent the enemy from capturing a man, and it had ended with the loss of so many more.

"Not every man is like that, Chloe," he said.

"I know," she said.

"I'm not like that."

She looked up, her eyes clashing with his. "I just… it's hard. Trusting. There are things I know in my mind, but…"

"Your body believes something different?" She nodded. "I know all about that," he said. "I know about forcing your body and brain to be completely separate. To want separate things."

"You don't ever feel, Sayid? Do you *want?*"

Sayid answered without thinking. He didn't know the answer until he spoke it. "People are born feeling," he said. "Born wanting. I had the ability to do so torn from me at an early age." A flash of Sura dressed in white, a veil over her face, entered his mind again. Of her being forced into a car, her screams carried over the wind… "Sometimes the desire for that, to have that back, that which other people simply…have, as innately as the instinct to breathe, is so strong I feel like it will consume me. I imagine the only thing more burdensome than feeling everything, is feeling nothing. Even when you want to."

Tears stung Chloe's eyes. She hadn't expected such an honest admission. "But surely you can… surely you…"

"I was trained to be a soldier, Chloe. To carry the dreams of others inside of me. Protect the expectations, the lives of others. There was no room to carry my own inside of me, too. A man in my position can't care for his own life, or he'll never be able to do what must be done. He cannot want. He cannot need. He cannot love. I had to be retrained. And I was, quite effectively."

"How?" she asked, her voice a whisper.

"Conditioning. When I gave in to a want, I was given pain in return. When I responded to the pain, more pain was administered. Until eventually, I learned to show nothing."

"No...Sayid, surely your parents wouldn't have allowed such a thing."

"My parents didn't raise me. My uncle did. And while it is easy to sit here and be horrified by the method, I cannot deny that in the end it saved my life. I would never have survived being a prisoner of war if not for that training. And if it had taken root a little stronger, I never would have been taken captive in the first place."

"Tell me," she said.

He wanted to. He wasn't sure why. "We were passing through a heavily forested area on our way to the enemy encampment to rescue men who had already been taken. Ours was meant to be a covert mission. No loss of life on either side if it could be helped. Alik Vasin was the tactical mastermind behind it, and Alik's intelligence never fails."

"What happened?"

"I failed. Because I saw two soldiers attempting to rape a woman and I moved out of hiding to stop them."

"And did you?"

"It was the last thing either of them did," he said, his tone grim. He didn't regret what he'd done to those men. He never would.

"Then what happened?"

"We were spotted. And many of my men were killed. More taken captive, including myself."

"Did the woman...did she escape?"

He nodded slowly. "She did."

"You did what you had to do. You did what any decent man would do."

"But I am not meant to be a decent man, *habibti,* I'm meant to be a soldier. I have to look at the big picture. Take action that causes the least damage, and I did not do that. Because of feeling."

She shook her head. "You had to."

"I should not have."

"I'm sure that woman doesn't think so."

"And what about the women whose husbands didn't come home to them because of that decision? What about them?"

Chloe looked down. "I don't know."

"That is my life, Chloe. The decisions I have to make. That is why I had to be made stronger, to be made into a man who acted logically, not emotionally."

"But what about what *you* want?"

"I don't even know what it might be."

"But you must have a goal...a place you see yourself going."

"I have always expected death on the battlefield. That Rashid should die first…that never entered my mind. That was my place. Not his. Never his."

"But you're a person, too, Sayid. A man."

"I'm a symbol," he said. "In much the same way my brother was, in much the same way Aden will be. But what I symbolize is different. I'm not the figurehead. I'm not the heart. I can have no weakness. I'm the strength. The merciless retribution. The protection. Beneath that, there is nothing. I *am* those things, and if I ever fail in it, my country will fail."

She looked into his eyes, into the voice, and she trembled. He was saying, with utter conviction, that what he was, all he was, was the man she had seen so far. That he was a machine, a tool, used to carry out the will of the country, of the people.

And in that moment, she saw the truth of it. Because there was nothing deeper in his eyes.

But there was the kiss. The kiss in the hall. The heat it had generated. And before that, there was the anger. It was there. She had to believe it was there.

"There is little merit to feeling, Chloe, you know that better than anyone. The temptation is there, of course it is. Because while not feeling cuts out pain, it also robs you of beauty. But look at the pain it can cause. Look at what it did to your home. To your parents."

She nodded slowly. "I know…I…"

"Six years ago, on that mission, I was taken as a prisoner of war. They held me for a year, before Alik

Vasin was able to find me and lead the rescue that saved my life. I was tortured. For three hundred and sixty-five days. Every day. In an attempt to break me. In an attempt to learn the secrets of Attar. An attempt to break Attar. The only thing that saved me, the only thing that kept me intact was the void. That deep, empty place inside of me that would have held another man's fear and pain. I was able to embrace the emptiness and endure it. It saved me."

And now it was killing him. She could feel it. Could feel the weight of all the dark matter inside of him. She wondered how he went on breathing.

He'd done what she'd tried to do. She'd escaped into books. Into science and logic, but she'd never cut herself off altogether. She'd limited relationships, stayed away from men and sex. But she'd never lost the desire for a connection. For love.

Looking at Sayid she was grateful for that. But then…she'd never been tortured.

"Sayid…I'm so sorry."

"Don't," he said. "I don't require pity."

"But I'm sorry," she said, knowing it was wrong, knowing it wasn't what she was supposed to say. But she was. So much. The image of him in so much pain gutted her. Destroyed her.

She felt all the things he couldn't feel for himself and it immobilized her. No wonder he shut it off. No wonder the void was better.

"Don't be," he said.

"Then what do you want?" she asked. "What do you need?"

He closed his eyes for a moment. "I don't know."

"How can you not know?"

He opened his eyes again. "It's never mattered."

But it had at some point. She knew it had.

"But surely you…I mean surely you've had some things you've…wanted. Lovers, and such."

"I've had lovers," he said. "How much I wanted them specifically is up for debate." A lie. If not a lie, incomplete information. She wasn't sure how she knew, only that she did. "You on the other hand…" He reached out and took a lock of her hair between his thumb and forefinger. "I can see a man getting lost in you."

"A man?"

"Yes."

"But not you?" He met her eyes. It was like staring into the blackness of space. "Oh, that's right."

He extended his hands, his thumb shockingly gentle on her cheek. "Tell me more about your life. How is it you and Tamara had such different upbringings? She spoke happily of her childhood."

"Tamara's mother left our father. Tamara was nearly ten years older than I am. Her mother wouldn't stand for the abuse. And mine would. Tamara never saw it because the first time he raised a hand to her mother, her mother walked away. And mine let him do it. Over and over again. She let him beat her unconscious because she couldn't bear the thought of being without him. He held her captive. Utterly captive by promising pleasure that matched the pain."

"That's why you get angry when I touch you."

And in that moment, Sayid was angry for her. For all she had seen. It wasn't necessary for her. She'd been an innocent, a child. She hadn't been born to it the same way he had been. She hadn't deserved it.

"I'm angry at myself," she whispered, the brokenness in her voice twisting his heart. "Because I could be her, Sayid, couldn't I? I could let a man have control over my body. That's why…you're right, in some ways. It is safer if you don't feel. I've always felt emotion but I've never…"

"You've never what?" he asked, his voice rough.

"I've always tried to make sure that my mind was stronger than my body," she said. "That I wasn't controlled by…passion."

Something hot and dark ignited in his stomach, a need to taste her passion. A need to help her set it free. A need to be at the mercy of it. The desire was so strong he felt weak with it. To simply take for a moment. To have no choice, for once, but to feel, rather than have to hold himself at a distance.

He looked at the silk scarf that was draped over her hair and lust kicked through his gut.

He extended his hand and took her chin between his thumb and forefinger, tilting her face up. "Then perhaps you need to control the passion."

CHAPTER TEN

CHLOE LOOKED UP AT SAYID, her pulse pounding. "What exactly do you mean?"

"That's up to you," he said, his tone rough. "But I want you to understand that you have power, too."

There was something strange in his voice, something tight. Something nervous. It made *her* nervous.

"What do you mean?" she asked.

"I am going to give you something" He gripped the end of the silk scarf that covered her hair and slid it off, running his fingertips over the smooth fabric.

"What?" she asked, her voice a choked whisper.

He wound the silk around his hands, drawing it tight between them. "Control."

"But you…you said yourself, you need it."

"I have never once willingly given it. But tonight, I give it to you." He let the scarf fall away from his left hand. "We can't spend the night in separate rooms," he said. "After tonight it won't matter. The royal couple never share a room full-time. But tonight, you know we have to."

She nodded. She didn't trust herself to speak. She

didn't want to. She wanted to hear what he would say, see what he would do. She was captivated, incapable of resisting.

He walked over to the closet and opened the doors. Her clothes were in there, along with some more traditional Attari garments that had been provided for her. He slid a red scarf off of its hook, wrapping it around his hand.

"Nothing will happen tonight that you do not desire. The power is yours." He placed both scarves at the foot of the bed, spread them out, then turned to her and tugged his shirt over his head. "My word to you. My promise. This is what I want, Chloe."

Her heart nearly stopped at the sight of his body. He was broad and muscular, dark hair scattered over his pecs and down washboard abs. She'd never seen a man that looked like him. When the science department had a pool party, the physiques usually ran from slim to doughy, with the color typically best described as fish-belly.

Not Sayid. He was hard, bronzed, utter masculine perfection. And she had no idea what to do with all that man.

"I don't…why did you take your shirt off?"

"Because, if you want to do it later, it will be difficult." He sat down on the edge of the bed and picked the scarves up, holding them out to her. She took a step forward and took them from him, running her thumb along the silken fabric.

He looked at her, his dark eyes intense. "I want you to tie my hands."

Her mouth dropped open, her heart slamming against her breastbone. "I...I can't...I don't...what are you...what are you asking me to do?" She thought of him, held captive, at the mercy of those who tortured him, who beat him, and then she thought of him asking her to bind him now. It filled her with a sense of total awe, the power he gave. The trust.

He was telling her to make a choice, forcing her to. To take responsibility for a part of her life rather than simply letting things happen to her. And she wanted to make the choice. Wanted to be the one in charge more than she'd realized.

He pushed himself back into the center of the bed, his muscles shifting and bunching. He put his hands out in front of him. "Tie my hands, and whatever happens after that, will be up to you."

Fear gripped her around the neck, putting pressure on her throat. That wasn't surprising. What surprised her was the desire that coiled in her stomach. The knot of lust that told her to do it. To tie his hands, and spend the night with him completely at her mercy. Hers to touch. Hers to explore.

"Think of it as a science experiment," he said, his voice husky, his eyes dark.

"I'm a theoretical physicist. I don't actually...do experiments. I...I think about how they work and make an equation. So, I would deduce maybe that me, plus you and these scarves would produce a possibly pleasurable outcome. And then I would…write it down."

"That doesn't sound very enjoyable."

"Perhaps not, but it's safe."

"Nothing in life is safe. I think where we are right now, what we did today, proves that."

She looked back down at the scarves. He was right. Nothing was safe. Plans fell apart. People died. There were no guarantees. A year ago, she'd been a student, trying to make ends meet, resolutely avoiding relationships, never planning on having children.

And now, she was here with Sayid. Married. A mother in every way that counted. And none of the things that she'd counted on to keep her safe had held. None of her plans, her oh-so-well-laid plans, had gone as she'd imagined.

She'd lived safe. She'd lived scared.

And none of it had been living.

These past weeks with Aden had been terrifying. And they had been rewarding in a way that she never could shave anticipated. The love she'd found with him went beyond words.

Then there was Sayid. The feelings he roused in her. The desire. The need. The ache that ran through her core made her want to strip off her every inhibition, made her feel more alive than ever before.

And she could embrace this now, or she could do what she'd always done. What she'd done before Aden. Before her life had changed forever. Or she could keep going forward.

She wrapped the silk around her hand, as he had done earlier, and let herself enjoy his body visually for a moment. Her breasts ached, a hard pulse beating at the apex of her thighs.

She knew about sex. She knew about it in a complete and scientific way, and she had seen it. Seen her parents during their "good" moments, when passion still ruled everything else.

But this really was a science experiment in many ways. A way to have him, while keeping him in a controlled condition. A way to harness his power, to experience it without setting it free.

"Lie back," she said, not quite recognizing her own voice. "And put your hands behind your head."

He complied, his movements slow, fluid, his dark eyes never leaving hers. He lay on his back, arms stretched above his head, each ridge of muscle clearly defined, each indrawn breath drawing attention to the perfect definition of his body.

"Are you sure you want to…to do this?"

"I am at your mercy," he said, black eyes unreadable.

She looked at him, looked into eyes that had seen such horror. "I swear to you," she said, "I won't do anything you don't want, either." It sounded silly, telling this big, strong man that she would take care of him. But she needed to say it. Needed him to know.

He nodded slowly, his eyes never leaving hers. She sucked in a breath and kneeled down on the edge of the bed, inching toward the center, toward him. She leaned over, then paused. "Kiss me?"

He complied, lifting his head and sliding his tongue over her lips, delving between them. She kissed him back, pouring her hunger, her anger, her fear, into this one act, giving him everything, everything she'd been carrying around inside of herself for so long.

They parted, their breathing harsh. She rested her forehead against his while she worked at getting her heart rate into a steady pace. She took the white scarf, wrapped the end of it around the bedpost, then wrapped the other end around his wrist, making sure the fabric rested flat against his skin.

"Is that okay?" she asked.

He tested the bonds. "Yes," he said, his voice strained. "Now the other one."

She repeated the action with the other bedpost and his other hand. "Test it?" He did, and the restraints held tightly. "Too much?" she asked.

He shook his head. "No."

She let out a long breath and looked at the man spread out before her. Yes, he could get up if he wanted to, could walk away. And that was important to her. Because even though she wanted the control, she didn't require total domination. She would never become what she despised.

"And now?" she asked.

"Whatever you want." And that was when she saw his need. His need for her to take the control, if only for a while. To lift the burden of it. To tie his hands and give him something other than the pain that life had offered him.

Which was just perfect, because, here and now, this was exactly what she needed.

"I don't know where to begin." She placed her hand flat on his chest, his skin hot beneath her palm. She'd never touched a man like this, had never explored the musculature of the male body.

Her fingers trembled as she slid them over his pecs, over his nipple. She swallowed hard. This was an experiment. Her chance to become familiar with a man's physical anatomy.

Yes, she could detach herself. Put it there, in the cerebral realm where things were logical and safe. She was a scientist. She was curious. And tonight, she would follow her curiosity where it took her.

Nothing more. Nothing less.

Science wasn't about emotion. It wasn't about fear. It was about finding facts. And that was what she was doing. Collecting facts.

"You're very…strong," she said, fingertips sliding over his abs. "In top physical condition."

He chuckled, the sound hoarse. "Am I?"

"Yes." She encountered scar tissue along his abdomen. "Oh…Sayid. You have scars."

"Lots of them," he said, and she knew he didn't just mean on his skin.

"You healed well," she whispered. At least on the outside. "If they were as severe as they appear to be."

"They were. And more."

"Yes. You're very strong." Stronger than any man should have to be.

"Are you planning on writing all this on your whiteboard?"

"Possibly."

"Why are you talking so much?"

"Because I don't know what else to do," she said, laughing, the sound nervous and unnatural. "I've never been in this position before." Let him think she only meant with a man tied up and at her mercy. And not just every single thing about the situation.

Until that moment in the hall, she'd never been truly kissed. And now...

Now she was here. But at least the pace would be up to her. How far things went would be up to her. But the scary thing was she didn't trust herself to stop. The body and brain disconnect at work again.

She leaned down and kissed his lips and he responded, then she abandoned his lips in favor of his neck, his chest. She pressed kisses to his muscles, feeling him stiffen beneath her, his muscles tensing, getting tighter.

"You like that?" she asked.

His only response was a grunt that she took as a yes. She slid down his body, tracing his abs with the tip of her tongue.

His body jerked beneath her.

"If my hands were free...." he said.

"But they aren't." She felt herself slipping in to

her role. Felt herself relishing the power. In taking some weight from him. In taking control of herself. Her life. "You're mine tonight."

She started to reach for his pants. She could see the outline of his erection, thick, much larger than she'd imagined. And she stopped. She wasn't ready for that, not quite yet.

Skin to skin. That was what she wanted. She reached behind her back and gripped the zipper tab for her dress, tugging it down and letting the bodice fall to her hips, then she quickly undid her bra leaving herself bare from the waist up.

It wasn't her nudity that filled her with insecurity, at least, not the part of it she'd imagined might bother her.

It was the fact that her stomach wasn't flat. That deep grooves, evidence of the life she'd carried inside of her, stretched over her entire midsection. It was the fear that it had been too long since she'd breastfed and she might embarrass herself.

"What are you thinking?" he asked.

"Um...what are you thinking?"

"I'm not," he said. "I can't think at all, not with you bared to me like this. Not when I'm finally seeing your breasts. Gorgeous."

"Men are easy to please," she said.

"In some ways."

"I'm glad about that." Because she didn't know any accomplished, practiced ways to please a man. And she found she did want to please him.

She took a breath and leaned forward, pressing her breasts against his chest. He took a breath and his chest hair scraped against her nipples, the friction sending a shock of pleasure through her body.

"I'm so sensitive there now," she said. "I never was before. But…oh, you feel so good."

"So do you."

She arched her back into him, moving back and forth, the stimulation sending waves of desire from the place where they made contact to the apex of her thighs. She was wet for him, the hollow ache widening inside of her. And she knew exactly what it would take to quench the ache, to fill the emptiness.

And then she was ready for him. To see him, touch him. Interesting, and something she would note later when her brain wasn't so fuzzy. Arousal, when intensified, seemed to decrease the ability to feel nervous.

She hooked her fingers in the waistband of his pants and dragged them down his legs. She paused for a moment just to look at him, to take in her first, up close and personal sight of a naked, erect man.

Chloe reached out and touched his shaft with the tip of her finger. He was hot. Hard. His skin surprisingly smooth. A harsh groan escaped his lips and his body jerked beneath hers again. He wanted free, she could sense it. But he hadn't asked. And she wouldn't offer.

Growing bolder, she wrapped her fingers around his length, squeezing him, gently at first, then more tightly. The tighter grasp earned her a sharp hiss of indrawn breath, his muscles so tight they shook.

"Like that?" she asked.

"Yes," he said, biting out a sharp curse. "Yes."

"I'm not very experienced at this," she said, glossing over the truth again.

"You're doing fine." She squeezed again. "Better than fine."

"Good." A shocking thought occurred to her, a craving she'd never imagined she might have. "Do you like it when a woman puts her mouth on you?"

"What?" he asked.

"Do you like oral sex?"

A harsh laugh escaped his lips. "Is there a man who doesn't?"

"I don't know. I told you, I don't have a lot of experience." She leaned in. "And I've never done this before."

"Chloe…"

She flicked her tongue over the head of his penis, the taste salty, and very much Sayid. She found she liked it. Found that she liked it almost as much as using him to stimulate her body. She cupped him in her hand, teasing his length with her tongue before drawing as much of him into her mouth as she could.

One hand was braced on his thigh and she could feel him shaking beneath her. Could feel how much it cost him to remain bound.

"Chloe," he said, his voice rough. "You need to stop."

"I don't have to, though," she said, "you're in my control."

"Chloe, do you have any idea how close I am?"

She knew what he meant. And she didn't want it to be over. But she didn't want to stop tasting him, either. Because the alternative was to go to the next stage and she wasn't certain she was ready for that, either.

"Chloe," he said, his tone pleading. "Kiss my lips."

She slid up his body, deciding to comply with this one demand, taking his mouth, feasting on it. "Scoot up," he said.

So she did. He lifted his head and captured the tip of her breast with his lips, his tongue flicking over her nipple.

"Careful," she said, pulling away. "There might be some unwanted consequences to that behavior at the moment."

She scooted away from him and shimmied the rest of the way out of her dress, leaving her in nothing more than a pair of white lace panties. Again, it was the idea of what her body looked like now. What it looked like to him.

She put her hand over her stomach, trying to hide some of the loose skin and stretch marks.

"Don't," he bit out. "Don't hide from me." She lowered her hand. "Take your panties off."

"I'm the one that's supposed to be in charge. No further than I want, remember?"

"Please," he said.

Pleasure flooded her, the desperation in his command a magic wand sent to wave away any of her insecurities. He didn't care about the stretch marks. He didn't care about the baby weight. She could see from the look on his face, and from the thick, insistent erection he was sporting, that he very much liked what he was seeing. That he was anticipating, greatly, what she would do next.

Well, so was she. "Since you asked so nicely." She gripped the sides of her panties and drew them down her legs, leaving herself completely bare, completely open to his gaze. Her entire body felt hot, flushed, excitement and nerves vying for equal place inside of her.

A decrease in fear is a direct response to an increase in arousal.

She called up her earlier findings and sucked in a sharp breath, crawling back onto the bed. She rested on her knees, surveying the man spread out before her, trying to decide what she wanted to do next. What she wanted to touch, to taste.

"You're thinking very hard," he said.

"I am. But there are a lot of choices here, and I want to make the right one."

"Why not make them all?" he asked, his voice strained.

A thrill shot through her. "An excellent idea."

She bent down, bracing her hands on either side of her legs, kissing his leg, running her tongue along his inner thigh. She skipped his erection this time, and it earned her a growl of frustration that she found oddly exhilarating.

She'd never had power in her life, not in any area outside the academic. Her mind had always held a certain amount of it, but her body had been weak. She'd been unable to protect her mother, unable to stop her father. But here and now, her body had power. And she was savoring it, relishing it, this rare, perfect moment when she felt whole. As though her body and brain were, for once, in agreement. Were equal.

She pressed a kiss to his abs, his chest, and then, her thighs on either side of his, her lips just a whisper from his mouth, she leaned in, letting her breath tease him, not touching. He arched up and she backed away, withholding her mouth from him.

He sat up, using his core muscles and pressed his lips to hers, holding the kiss for as long as possible before he lay back down, his breath coming in harsh pants.

"Tease," he ground out.

"I am, I guess. I hadn't realized." She leaned in and ran her tongue along the line of his jaw, nipping his chin.

"Chloe, please," he said. There was no undertone of begging in his words. They were harsh, raw, desperate. And even in her inexperience, she knew exactly what he wanted.

She only hoped she knew how to give it, that she was ready to give it.

She pressed her body against his, the hard ridge of his arousal coming into contact with her clitoris. She hissed out a breath as sparks shot through her.

The theory held. Arousal, need, made her brave.

He was big, but she'd given birth, so this was hardly the place for virginal nerves of that nature. It was more the fear of the unknown, of what might happen. How it would change things.

But nothing in her world was the same as it had been a year ago. Nothing felt the same as it had even two months ago.

One more change. One more new thing.

But at least this one was her decision. At least it was something she wanted. So many things in life had simply happened to her, but not this. She was choosing this. She wanted this. She wanted Sayid.

"I want you," she said, speaking it, making it real. This was for her. She wanted him, and she would have him. Him, and not fear. Pleasure, and not images of violence and pain. The touch of another human being, closeness. Desire. She could have it, when she'd never before let herself believe that she could.

"Take me."

She sucked in a breath and reached behind her back, shifting her hips and guiding his erection into her body. She was wet, and it eased the way in as he filled her, stretched her. She winced, a couple of tender places making themselves felt. He flexed his hips, burying himself inside of her completely.

She gripped his shoulders, her nails digging into his flesh, her breath stalled out as she tried to acclimate to the invasion on her body, as she tried to process the pleasure, pain and utter feeling of possession.

It took a moment, but the pain faded, leaving a feeling of fullness, intense, wonderful fullness behind.

"Oh…yes," she breathed. "This is good."

He flexed his hips, his pelvis pressing against her clitoris, sending another shower of pleasure through her. She moved against him, finding that perfect point of contact again, giving herself another dose of that addicting sensation.

"Lift your hips up," he said.

The instruction was appreciated. She obeyed, his command, the friction of his shaft sliding out of her heightening her pleasure, the motion pushing the sensitive bundle of nerves against his body when she came back down.

She repeated the move again and again, finding a rhythm that tightened the coil of need that rested low in her stomach to an unbearable level. Until she was certain it would break her. Until she was sure she couldn't endure it anymore.

She quickened her pace, urgency, desperation, pushing toward an end that was nothing more than a shapeless void in her mind. She didn't know what she was chasing, only that she needed it more than she needed her next breath.

And then the tension shattered, tiny shards of pleasure bursting through her. She raked her nails down his chest, over his abs, as her release dug into her, holding her captive, making it impossible to think or breathe, to do anything but simply ride the wave as it broke over her, to give herself over utterly, completely to the physical world. There was no reason here, no logic, no cold buffer of fact and science to make her an observer.

Then he thrust his hips hard, a harsh sound escaping his lips, his chest muscles contracting beneath her hands as his own orgasm took him over. She bent and took his mouth, catching every last sound of release on her tongue. And it consumed her. Utterly. Completely. It was passion, in its most raw, undiluted form.

And she didn't fear it. Instead, she let it take her under.

CHAPTER ELEVEN

Sayid worked at catching his breath. He couldn't. He was certain his heart was about to pound out of his chest. His wrists were still bound, the muscles in his chest, back and shoulders aching now from being tied so tightly for so long.

He had been bound before. Chained to a wall and beaten. Unable to move while knowing that unendurable pain was about to touch him. Bound up inside of himself, unable to vent the pain, the anguish that he felt, watching the woman he loved being ripped from the only life she knew, being torn away from him. Watching his men falling around him.

It was impossible to say what had driven him to allow himself to be tied down again. To put himself at the mercy of another person. Somewhere inside of him there had been a dark desire to taste captivity again. Captivity at her hands this time. To prove to himself that if he were bound again, it wouldn't always be pain he was waiting for. That it could be a pleasure.

To simply allow himself to be, rather than having to keep such a tight reign on himself at all times. To challenge what he had been taught. To see what might happen if he tried once again to give up some control.

Now he knew. Knew that when he dreamed of his wrists being bound, he wouldn't be waiting for the crack of a whip, but the slow wet slide of Chloe's tongue on his skin.

He ached to hold her now. A strange need, one he'd not felt in years. But his shields were down. Not forever, but for the moment, surrendered to this woman, along with his control.

His hands were still bound, preventing him from following through.

"Chloe," he said, the roughness of his own voice shocking him.

She lifted her head, her blue eyes wide, dazed. "Yes?"

"Can you untie my hands?"

"You said I could keep you that way all night."

"Are you still afraid of me?" he asked. He held his breath while he waited for the answer.

"No," she said slowly. "I like you like this, though."

"I'm not opposed to it," he said. "At least not under these circumstances. But I think my right shoulder is starting to lose feeling."

"Oh!" She scrambled up his chest, naked and lush, and started working at the ties on his wrists.

When he was free, he had to fight the instinct to

pull her into his arms and roll her beneath him, to feel those curves pressed against him again.

But he wouldn't do that to her. Not now. Not after what had passed between them.

"Can I?" he asked, drawing near to her.

She nodded, not asking exactly what he wanted from her. He wrapped his arms around her, pulling her against his chest, like he'd been dying to do. He ran his hands over her curves, her waist, the luscious curve of her butt.

"I needed to touch you," he said. "So soft. Was it a successful experiment for you?"

She laughed softly, burying her head in his chest. "It's not really conclusive. You have to test findings. Try to disprove them. It has to be repeated in a controlled environment."

"Repeated?" His body was very much interested in the idea, although his bruised and battered insides wondered if they could stand the experience.

He'd never felt anything like the release he'd just had. Had never had anything run so deeply inside of him. Had never been filled by such a profound sense of connection. For one moment, as he'd been inside of her, his release roaring through his ears, he'd felt weightless. He'd felt as if he'd seen himself. The man he might have been, if he had not spent his lifetime being trained to be someone different. Had he not had all of the desires in him stripped away, hollowed out.

It had been a surrender for him. Unexpected. Necessary.

He'd felt as if his body was caving in on itself, had felt as though he was ready to disappear entirely, crushed by all that he suppressed. By all of the things he denied, held down deep inside, that he simply wasn't allowed to feel. Things he didn't know how to release. Things he never could release.

But she'd given him a moment's peace. A moment more than he'd ever had before.

"For science," she said, her tone comically serious.

"You're very dedicated to your work," he said drily, lying down and bringing her with him, his arms still wrapped around her body.

"I really am." She put her hand on his chest, slender fingers moving idly over his skin. "I guess we made the marriage really, really legal."

"I suppose so."

"Oh! Dammit!" She sat upright, the sound of Aden stirring.

"What?" he asked.

"I'll be right back." She grabbed a robe from out of the closet and threw it on, scurrying from the room.

She returned a few moments later with Aden in her arms, and sat down in the chair by the vanity. "Sorry. Could hear him crying." She swept her robe aside and put the baby to her breast. He was powerless to do anything but watch. To watch the way she cared for him. And he understood then, why she'd given up everything. Because she was Aden's mother in every way. In the only way that mattered.

A scream tore through his insides, ravaging him. Because he would never be Aden's father. He would never be Chloe's husband. Not really.

Desire, sweet, bitter desire, stabbed at his chest. Not for her body, but for something altogether more serious. Something he couldn't have. Ever. It was a brief moment, but the strength of it, the intensity, shook him deep. It took that moment of watching the woman he loved sent to marry another and made that pain a pale shadow, eclipsed by the longing he felt now.

It was such a painful vision. A strange, melting haze of his past and future. Sura. The baby she hadn't been allowed to give birth to. His baby.

When he'd found out she was pregnant, he had imagined a scene like this. He had been happy. Overjoyed. And then it had all been stripped from him, piece by piece, until this image was one burned into his brain as something he couldn't have.

Never.

Tonight could never happen again. His defenses were down and they weren't going back up easily. His chest throbbed, the desire for something, for more than he had, more than he would ever have, tearing at him.

No. Tonight could never happen again.

Chloe had spent the night in bed with Sayid, but he hadn't done what she'd expected. He'd been so warm after they'd made love, so affectionate almost. She'd never been touched so much in her life, not in love, not in anger. She'd simply never been close to anyone.

But after she'd fed Aden and taken him back to the nanny, he'd changed. The wall back up between them. They had slept, and that was all.

She'd ended up putting her foot against his calf in an effort to maintain some of the intimacy that had been created between them.

Now she was wandering around the palace, wearing Aden in a sling, trying not to drown in confusion.

She was a such a typical female. And she'd spent so many years avoiding it! But now she was doing that thing, that thing that women did. She was on the slippery slope.

What had it meant to him? Would they do it again? Had it been as good for him as it had been for her?

Maybe if she hadn't been a virgin it wouldn't be such a big deal. She'd never really liked thinking of herself that way. Mainly because it sounded saintly or something and she'd never imagined herself that way. She'd simply elected not to go the route of acquiring physical relationships.

A flash from last night hit her hard. Sayid deep inside of her, his eyes hungry, his hands bound. It sent a shiver through her, a deep longing to have him inside of her again. And again. And again.

Yes, staying away from physical relationships had been her plan. It had probably been the best plan going for her. But she'd ruined it now. Now she'd been with Sayid. Now she knew.

More than that, she'd seen inside of him. Seen the depth of the cavern in his soul. The emptiness. It froze her inside. Terrified her. Made her feel as if she was standing on a ledge, looking down into endless nothing.

Part of her was afraid of falling in. Part of her wanted to jump.

All of her wanted to avoid him for a little longer. And she'd managed to since he'd left her room early that morning. It was afternoon now, the sun low in the sky, casting a burnished orange flame onto the sea, the reflection shining in through the window, painting the white rock walls in the same color.

"Sheikha."

Chloe looked up and saw Sayid standing in front of her, his broad frame filling the corridor. Her heart lifted into her throat before free-falling into her stomach.

"Sheikh," she returned, knowing her tone didn't possess half of the cool sophistication that was inherent in his.

"I trust you are well rested?"

He was going to act as though nothing had happened between them. There was no innuendo in his tone, no knowing look. She deserved a knowing look. She deserved some innuendo, at the very least. "Indeed. I trust that you don't have any rope burn?"

She could have bitten off her tongue.

He arched one dark brow. "I seem to be intact."

"Nice for some."

"Chloe, what happened last night must not be repeated."

"Why not?" she asked, still horrified at the words coming out of her mouth. Unable to stop them. "Because it wasn't good for you? You didn't like having sex with me because I have stretch marks? Or was it because I was a virgin who didn't have a clue about what she was doing? You know, it's really daunting to be presented with a naked man and be told to have at it when you've never—"

"A what?" he asked, his tone soft. Ice-cold.

"A...a virgin."

"You've had a child!" he said.

"I don't see why it's that surprising. You know how I conceived him."

"I'm sorry, I must have missed the star in the East. Maybe if I'd seen it I would have felt like I had adequate warning."

"So, it is a problem."

"Yes!" he roared. "No. That's not why it can't happen again."

"Then why not?"

"Because you're not my damned wife!"

"Oh. I...well, yeah, I am, actually," she said, blinking.

"You're my wife on paper," he said, lowering his voice. "But I do not wish to confuse our relationship this way."

"Oh, I see, and now you can claim I tied you down and forced you? Sorry, Sayid, but you can't. I don't buy it. And no one else would, either. You had plenty of time to say no last night."

"I didn't want to. But I knew I should have. I knew it never should have gone so far, and I let it anyway. More reasons why it can't happen again. And you were a virgin." He swore.

"Yeah, I know. You're the only one of the two of us that's surprised by that one. I was actually very aware of the fact."

"A fact you should have made me aware of."

"Or what? It wouldn't have happened? Then I'm really glad you didn't know, because I needed it to happen. And actually, I needed it to happen in just that way. You let me have the control, you made me take it, and I don't think I've ever done that before. No, I know I haven't."

"Of course you have," he said, his tone dismissive. As if he needed to dismiss what had passed between them. "You're on your way to a doctorate, you've hardly been inactive."

"Yes, okay, academically, I've done things. A lot of things. But that's easy. It's easy for me to take control there, to be in charge. But I…I've lived in my head, Sayid. And Aden…Aden started forcing me to consider my body. To be connected with the physical part of myself. To realize that I'm a woman, not just a disembodied brain. And you…you made me make a choice, rather than just going along with life. Rather than just being afraid. And I did. Don't ask me to regret it."

"I don't need you to regret it."

"But you do. You regret it."

"I should," he said, his voice rough.

"Why?"

"Because I am not the man for you. I'm not the man for a virgin."

"Oh, for heaven's sake, Sayid, you act like I was some innocent, and I most certainly wasn't that. I'd never been with a man before, but that was my choice. I know about sex. I've given birth, as you pointed out. I watched my mother get beaten until she was unconscious, until she bled. I've lived through the death of my half sister, the only family I could stand to be around, before I really got to know her. And I've had to fight to keep the child that I think of as mine, even though, biologically, he isn't. Even though logically I shouldn't. So don't you dare treat me like I'm breakable. Don't you dare try to protect me. I know you're a product of violence. Well, so am I. I don't have any innocence in me. No, I'd never had sex before, but that doesn't mean I'm naive enough to look at life, or you, with rose colored glasses—" she sucked in a sharp breath "—and you made a mistake assuming I would even want to. I'm as pleased about this marriage being temporary as you are, and a little sex isn't going to change that."

"You think not?"

"I think not," she returned.

"You think you want me? Every night? In your bed?"

She swallowed hard, nodding. "As long as it suits us both." She wasn't sure why she'd said that, wasn't sure why she was giving in. She should tell him it was one and done. Should tell him he could never touch her again. She shouldn't want him to touch her again. But she did.

"What about with my hands unbound?" He reached out, his thumb skimming her cheekbone. "What about then? When I can bend you over the bed, like I fantasized about. When I can grip your hips tight while I go deep inside you. What about then?"

She swallowed, her throat dry. "Yes. Then." She wasn't sure what was making her so brave, why she wasn't shrinking away from his words.

She looked hard into those dark, fathomless eyes. She knew why. Sayid said he felt nothing, but she knew, knew for a fact, that that was a lie. It was a lie he told himself, as much as one he told the world. A lie he believed with every piece of himself.

There was more to him than he believed. More than he knew.

And she knew one thing for her. She could trust him. As far as how he would handle her physically, she could trust him.

"Yes," she said. "You would never abuse me. You would never hurt me. You would never use my desire for you as a punishment. You would never use it to bend me to your will. And you wouldn't use your fists to do that, either. Tell me I'm wrong."

"Chloe…"

"You can't. Because I'm not wrong. I'm right, and you know it. I'm not afraid of you," she said, taking a step toward him, putting her palm flat on his chest. "I don't need to be."

"I would never hurt you physically, Chloe. Never. But I could hurt you in other ways. I will never love you. I can't."

"Who said I wanted that? I didn't. In fact, I think I said the opposite. I think I said that I don't need forever. And I don't. I just want this. For as long as we can have it. Until it burns out. I've never been able to have this before. I've never wanted it. I've always been so scared. I just let…life, the past, sort of kick me along the stream. I worked hard in my professional life, but when it comes to relationships, I've never tried."

"You've tried with Aden."

"He's the first person. Ever. The first person I've ever felt truly bonded to." It would have happened with Tamara, but they'd never had the chance. And now she felt it with Sayid. She would call it a side effect of the sex, but she could remember feeling this exact feeling at the wedding, as the vows were spoken.

She didn't want to analyze it. Not closely, not even at a distance. She just wanted the physical. For once, she just wanted to let go of thought and do what felt good.

And it was freeing. To let herself loose, to let herself embrace a part of herself she'd shoved down so deep she hadn't realized it existed.

"I do want you, Sayid," she said. "For as long as we both want each other. Do you think you can handle me?"

He chuckled, a low, humorless sound. "*Habibti,* I am not the one you should have concern for."

"You never know."

"You're trying to see something in me that doesn't exist."

"Maybe," she whispered, realizing the truth of it when she spoke it.

"Don't," he said. "Understand this, I didn't experience a little trauma in prison and come out like this. I was like this when I went in. The reason I survived is because this was the man I was when they captured me. I would throw myself on a bomb tomorrow to save a life, and it's not because I'm so brave, or so heroic. It's because I don't genuinely see any future for myself, neither do I have a care for it. And it's because I feel nothing. Because nothing means a damn thing to me."

The admission chilled her, terrified her. And part of her refused to believe it. She hated that part of herself, even as she clung to it. She had to believe there could be better for him. That there could be more.

She strode forward, keeping space between their bodies, one hand on Aden's back, curling her arm around Sayid's neck and going up on her tiptoes, kissing him, fiercely, possessively. He planted his hands on her hips, kissing her back, tracing her lips with his tongue before delving in deep.

When they parted, they were both breathing hard. She rested her forehead against his and closed her eyes, trying to make sense of the emotion coursing through her body.

"Do me a favor, Sayid," she said.

"What?" he asked, his voice husky.

"Don't throw yourself on a bomb anytime soon. You might not care, but I do."

He didn't speak for a moment, didn't move. "Do me a favor, Chloe," he said finally.

"What?"

"Don't care. Not about me."

It was too late for that. "I'll do my best."

CHAPTER TWELVE

SAYID HAD NEVER BEEN accused of being reckless. He was a planner, a strategist, and while he took risks, they were always calculated.

But with Chloe, he had been reckless.

He had missed the signs of her innocence, and he was nearly certain it wasn't because she'd hidden it so carefully. It was simply because he hadn't wanted to see it. Because what he'd wanted, what he'd needed, was to lose himself in her, to take advantage of the crack she'd put in those self-imposed walls. To allow himself a moment to breathe, unrestricted, unbound.

He'd only been with a virgin once before, and never would have sought one out again. He was the wrong man for such a task.

He had cared about Sura. Had loved her. But he'd been a different man then. A boy, really. Sixteen and, though he'd been affected by his uncle's child rearing tactics, he was not yet broken. The two of them had shared in first love, their first time together a meeting of hearts, not simply of bodies.

But that boy he'd once been was dead, along with
the capability to love as he once had. It had not been
his heart that had craved Chloe. He'd used her. Used
her as a way for him to break free of his demons.
Sure, he'd wrapped it up in giving her control, giving her something she needed, and while he knew
it had worked for her, it had been a selfish act in
many ways.

One he was actively attempting to regret, but
could not. He was also trying to forget her offer in
the hall. The offer to be with him, for as long as they
both desired.

He wanted it. Wanted it much more than he should.

He raked his fingers through his hair and stared
out at the sea from the window of his office. He
could hardly recognize himself. He felt like he was
in another man's body. A body that was starting to
ache, to tingle, like muscles and nerves long unused
were waking up. Were regaining feeling.

It terrified him, how much he wanted it to happen. How much he wanted to stop it.

He threw his mind back. To the beatings Kalid had
given him. Beaten him until he had learned to stop
screaming. Until he'd found a way to make himself
hold the pain in.

To the loss of the one person he'd loved, the tiny
life he'd scarcely gotten a chance to love.

That was why he couldn't feel. Why he must never
feel.

He felt like the office walls were curving inward,

closing in on him. Like a prison. A gilded prison, one that forced him to hide himself. Only, he was finding little sanctuary within today. Bit by bit, the crown was breaking through his defenses. And Chloe was accelerating the destruction.

He pushed back from his desk and went down the stairs, stripping off the long jacket he was wearing, the one that denoted his rank. He stripped his shirt off, too. Edged in gold, the dark blue symbolizing royalty. He wanted none of it today.

The sun was, as ever, close to the earth in Attar, even as it sunk into the sea, the rays searing his skin, the cool ocean breeze coming behind it to wash away the sting. Sayid walked out onto the beach, looked out at the horizon, endless and open, the gray and green waves rolling back toward the sky in an infinite motion. And still he felt trapped.

He had left the office, stripped off his royal garments and still he felt locked up tight. He would strip off his skin if it were possible. It was suffocating him.

He walked to the rocks that seemed to grow straight from the sand and leaned against the rough surface, the cutting pain in his back a familiar one at least.

It reminded him of being in jail. And it made the suffocation make sense at least.

If he couldn't make it go away, then maybe he could at least think of the place he'd truly been held captive and apply it to that.

His only other option was to recognize that it was his own body choking the life out of him.

"Sayid?"

He looked up and saw Chloe, stumbling over the sand, the wind whipping through her coppery hair, her short, cotton dress blowing up over her knees.

"What are you doing here, Chloe?"

"I saw you come down here."

"Where's Aden?"

"Sleeping. And the nanny is with him."

"So you thought you'd follow me? I thought I'd frustrated you enough this afternoon that you might avoid me."

She came to stand in the shadow of the rock, the stone shielding her from the wind, her hair tumbling over her shoulders. "I thought we settled this. Earlier today, in fact."

"You don't know what you're asking for, little virgin."

"Not a virgin anymore. And don't do that. Don't try to make it seem like I somehow don't understand things simply because I'd never had sex. I know the mysteries of the universe, sex hardly rocked my world."

"Did it not?" he asked, extending his hand and brushing his thumb over her cheek. He found he was addicted to the sensation of touching her that way. An illicit dose of her soft skin beneath his hand. Just a taste of what it had been to touch her naked body. And he hadn't done nearly enough touching that night. Not nearly enough.

"Well, in some ways it did." She looked down, a blush staining her cheek, dark enough for him to see, even in the falling twilight.

"Chloe, you should go back."

"No. Let me tell you something, Sayid al Kadar, you might be out of touch with your emotions, but I'm not out of touch with mine. I know what I want."

"And you want me? What a waste of your desire."

"It's not. How could it be? I'm your wife after all."

"Not my real wife," he said, his voice cold. "You will never be my wife in any real sense. Even now, even with you as my wife for this brief period of time, it puts you in danger, do you not see that?"

"I don't feel very in danger, actually. Which is funny, because I used to think that if I ever let a man get close to me…I would feel afraid. But you don't make me feel afraid."

"I should. As far as the world is concerned, you're my wife and that means you're vulnerable to an attack on me."

"I don't feel all that vulnerable when I'm with you. I feel strong."

She moved forward, and as she got closer, he felt the tightness around his body loosen. Felt himself start breathing again, truly.

"You could not stand against men like I've encountered."

"Is Attar at war right now?"

"No."

"Is there even a rumor of it?"

He shook his head. "Since my capture and return, all has been quiet. The message Alik Vasin delivered to our enemies after my rescue was…it had deep impact."

"Then that's not really what you're worried about."

"I know the reality of what can happen to a man in the hands of those who are truly evil. Can you imagine what they might have done if I'd had a weakness to exploit? If I had cared a bit for my own skin? Or for the skin of another." He put his hand on her cheek again, resting his palm there.

"So you'll simply go through life caring for no one?"

"It's all I can do now, Chloe, I don't think you fully understand. I can't do anything more. I was not trained to be a man, but a machine. And it's too late to undo it."

She stepped into him, kissing him, in the way that only Chloe could. Deep, inexperienced but filled with passion. Chloe didn't hold back.

"Another experiment, Chloe?" he asked, when they parted, his voice thick with lust.

She shook her head. "No. This isn't science."

"I thought you wanted everything to be scientific. To be able to explain it all."

"I don't want to explain this. I just want to feel it."

She wrapped her arms around his neck, and he encircled her waist with his, pulling her tightly against him, relishing the feeling of her lush breasts against his chest, relishing the chance to move his hands over her curves.

He could feel the chains falling off. Could feel the walls crumbling, a rush of fresh air moving through his soul.

He could breathe.

"Chloe," he said, her name a tortured sound on his lips.

He hands shook as he sifted his fingers through her hair and angled her head so he could delve deeper, sweeping the moist recess of her mouth with his tongue, tasting the essence of her, tasting Chloe, deep, letting her flavor fill him.

But it wasn't enough.

"Are you okay?" he ground out, wrenching his mouth from hers and searching her face for signs of fear.

She nodded. "I'm fine. As long as you don't stop."

"No chance, *habibti*."

"Good."

He tugged the top of her sun dress down and exposed her breasts. He looked back, saw that the palace was obscured from view by the rock. "No one will see," he said, his voice rough, another man's voice, filled the kind of animal need and desire he'd never allowed himself to feel.

"I hadn't even thought about it," she said, a shaky laugh injecting a tremor into her words.

He lowered his head and swept his tongue over her nipple, then the other.

"Careful about how you do that," she said.

He ignored her, tasting her again. Would he ever get enough? It seemed like the void had opened back up again, only now it was desperate to be filled by this. Hunger, need and lust. And Chloe. Always Chloe.

"Sayid," she said.

"Oh, Chloe, I was missing a lot when I wasn't able to touch you," he said, sliding his thumb over one erect nipple. He lifted his head so that he could look at her, her face, filled with desire, his body flushed pink, further evidence of her arousal.

"I was missing quite a bit too."

"Let me show you how much," he said.

He moved his hands down around her back, sliding his fingertips along the elegant line of her spine, down to the rounded curve of her butt, still covered by the dress. He lifted the skirt up, sliding his fingertips beneath her panties, sucking in a harsh breath when he touched soft, bare skin. He squeezed her tight, loving her curves. Loving that she was all woman. Everything any man could possibly desire.

She shivered and he captured her trembling lip between his teeth as he moved his hand toward her inner thighs, his fingers coming into contact with the moisture between her legs.

"You want me," he growled.

"Yes," she whispered.

"Tell me," he said, needing to hear it, his body crying out to be filled by something. By feeling. "Tell me how much. Tell me what."

"It hurts how badly I want you," she whispered, burying her face in his neck, pressing a kiss to his throat.

"Tell me what you want," he said, sliding his fingers deeper, across the seam of her body, the evidence of her desire coating his skin.

"I want you," she panted, "I want you inside of me."

"Like this?" he asked, pushing one finger into her slick channel.

"More," she said, her voice shaking.

"This?" He added a second, working them in and out of her. She arched into him, her bare breasts rubbing against his chest. And he thought he would explode then and there. Thought his heart would burst from his body, thought he would come just from witnessing her pleasure. From feeling it.

Not yet.

He needed more.

He withdrew from her and she sagged against him. "Oh…"

"We aren't through yet." He reversed their positions, pressing her back against the rock. "Does that hurt?" he asked.

She shook her head.

"Good." He lowered himself in front of her, his

knees in the sand, a position of reverence. All the better to give her body the attention it deserved.

He gripped the bunched up fabric of her dress and tugged it down her hips, letting it fall to the ground. He leaned in, pressing a kiss to her stomach, just above the waistband of her panties.

She pushed her fingers through his hair, holding on tightly as he shoved her underwear down, leaving her completely exposed. Just as he wanted her.

He kissed her stomach again and she trembled. "You are so beautiful," he said. He brushed his fingertips over the lines on her stomach, evidence of all that carrying Aden had cost her. Physical proof. "I once thought of you as a mother tiger. And you are indeed. You've earned these stripes, and I am in awe of them. Of what they represent."

"They're…ugly."

"They aren't." He kissed one of the lines, giving proof to his words. "You are beautiful everywhere."

He moved his lips down. "Absolutely everywhere," he said against her skin.

Then he kissed her at the bundle of nerves at the apex of her thighs, sliding his tongue along the same path his fingers had taken earlier. Her fingers tightened in his hair, incoherent sounds escaping her lips as he pleasured her, tasted her, let himself be filled with her.

But it still wasn't enough.

He was so hard it hurt, but it wasn't his body that

felt the greatest need. It was the cavern inside of him where his soul should be.

He had never thought emptiness could hurt. But it did. In immeasurable ways.

"I need you now, Chloe," he said.

"Take me," she said.

He stood quickly, gripping her thigh, hooking her leg over his hip as he shoved his pants down his legs. He pushed into her, a raw groan coming from deep inside.

"Okay?" he asked.

She nodded, her eyes never leaving his. He thrust into her again, deep, hard. Over and over, the motion filling him, filling the void. He lowered his head, pressing a kiss to her shoulder, his eyes tightly shut as he chased the pleasure that was building inside of him, as he chased the feeling of being complete.

Of being whole.

A body at one with his mind. A body with a soul. Because he wanted Chloe with all of himself, with nothing held back in reserve. Nothing pushed down deep or hidden behind a wall. Every defense was demolished. And he relished it.

"Oh," she panted, her nails digging into his shoulders. "Oh, yes."

And he felt her internal muscles tighten around him, her orgasm washing through her, her pleasure pushing him to the brink, stealing his control, leading him over the edge of a cliff. The roar of blood in his ears was deafening, the intensity and power of his release so strong, so all-consuming that it shoved all of the pieces of himself together, holding them tight.

And in that moment he was home. He was Sayid, as he was meant to be. Body, mind and heart. And he felt. Felt so much that he thought he might die of it.

Like a bandage had been torn from him, leaving him to hemorrhage, to bleed out, a crimson stain on the sand.

He pulled her tightly against him, and sank to the ground, still buried deep inside of her. He wound his fingers through her hair, kissing her face, her neck, unable to do anything but touch her, to live in the moment, this one perfect moment.

Because he knew for certain that it couldn't last.

That he could not allow it.

Chloe couldn't believe she fell asleep, naked in the sand, shielded by the rocks, and by Sayid's arms. It was dark when she woke up, the air still thick and warm, bright stars dotting the sky.

It was so different here. So wild, so open. It made her want to match. Made her want to embrace wildness, to embrace life in a way she never had before. In that moment, Attar felt like home. Most especially with Sayid at her back, his body warm hard against hers.

"Sayid?"

"You are awake."

"Yes," she said. "I guess I... Well, I mean, I guess

it's common for orgasm to make people sleep but I'm still surprised I fell asleep on the beach."

"Oh, Chloe. Always reasoning."

"Not so much with you."

"I find I am the same."

"At least it isn't just me." Silence fell between them. "What happened?" she asked.

"What do you mean?"

"Before the prison. Before the...before you lost your men. You told me that you went in the man you are now. And I want to know what...happened."

"I was raised to be a man of war, and that means I was treated with little softness."

"And that's it? That's the beginning and end of it? I was raised by two people who didn't care whether or not I was even there, and I..."

"You aren't like me?"

"No. I tried to be. I tried to reason it all out, to stay away from emotion and passion but...it's in me and I can't stop it from coming out. And now I don't even want to."

"Because you love Aden," he said. There was a firmness to his tone, as though he was afraid she might mean that she cared for him. Too bad that she did. And she didn't even care not to, even if it meant she would get hurt.

Another decision. One borne of her own desire, rather than fear.

"Yes," she said. "And you can't. And I want to know why."

He was silent for a moment. She felt him take a breath, his chest expanding, his arms tightening around her. "This is not something I speak of."

She nodded. "I know."

"And yet you ask."

"Because I think you need to speak of it. I don't talk about my parents but…I told you. And I feel…I don't know, something feels like it's starting to heal."

"There were wounds that don't heal, Chloe. Wounds that simply become more scars."

"Please."

"I told you, my uncle, Kalid, raised me. From the time was seven, I lived with him. There were times he would subject me to pain, to numb my senses, my connection with my own body. Because I would need the detachment. The strength. He kept me separate from other children. From photos of my family, anything he thought might make me weak. He took me to the desert, to live with the bedouin people. It's an environment that forces you to become tough. But it was there that I found my greatest weakness. Her name was Sura."

She wanted to stop him for a moment, a wild surge of jealousy shooting through her, making her want to close her ears off to a story about the woman he had wanted. The woman who was a part of stealing his heart, not just in the normal way a lover stole it, but forever. Leaving the man she wanted for herself unable to return her feelings.

But she didn't. She forced herself to listen. To understand.

"I was a boy when we met. We were both twelve. And I wanted her to be mine forever. Wanted to protect her, to keep her. She became my best friend. She kept me from falling into the darkness after my uncle's beatings, kept me…feeling. And she was beautiful. So beautiful. When we were sixteen…I knew I loved her." He paused for a moment before continuing. "But my uncle wasn't stupid, and neither was her father. And it turned out, no great detective work was required to uncover my relationship with her. Not after she got pregnant."

Chloe was holding her breath now, an ache building in her chest that was threatening to shatter her. There would be no happy ending to this story.

"I was so happy when I found out about the baby. We were young but…I imagined that I had found a way to cheat the system I was in. To find a way out of the bleak, miserable hell. But it was my destiny, Chloe, what I was born for. And you cannot fight that. You can't beat it."

"What happened?" she asked, her voice a choked whisper.

"They took her to a clinic in the city, as soon as her father found out, and they terminated the pregnancy. Then it was a simple matter of selling her off to a neighboring tribal leader who didn't mind taking on damaged goods for a wife, so long as she was young and beautiful."

She felt Sayid's body shudder beneath her hands. "She screamed for me, Chloe, and they held me down. Held my hands so I couldn't move."

Chloe felt a tear slide down her cheek. "No…"

"Yes. They held me until…I broke free. And then one of Sura's father's men hit me in the back of the head with the butt of his gun and…that was all. It was not all my uncle, you understand. Sura's father didn't want me for his daughter. A marriage agreement had already been struck with the man she was sent to. But I know it was a lesson Kalid delighted in teaching me. And it was his ultimate triumph. There was nothing more to lose after that. And when you have nothing left…"

"Oh…Sayid…I… How did you endure it?"

"How could I not? She got much worse than I did, because she cared for me. That, if nothing else, reinforced my place in life." He breathed in deeply. "When I gained control over the Attari army, after Kalid's death, the first thing I did was send them to rescue her."

"You didn't go?"

He shook his head. "I had nothing for her anymore."

"And…was she okay?"

"She was happy. Her first husband had died, and she had since met a man who took her to live in the city. But those years she suffered…I will never forgive the men involved. For the loss of my child. For what they did to Sura, for the pain that she endured all because she loved me." He sucked in a sharp breath. "I was foolish. I had thought that I could be the man I was meant to be, and still have love. A wife. Children. It was a pain that brought me to my knees. I was choked with it. When I found out she was to be given to someone else…" His voice broke then, the pain evident. "It was my fault, Chloe. Kalid told me. If I hadn't…if I hadn't shown such weakness…I showed my hand. I showed my weak spot. I made her a target. And that day I vowed I would never show weakness again. More than that, I would never feel it."

"Easier than grieving," she said.

"Easier than one day, watching a wife be taken by an enemy. Watching them do to her what was done to me in the prison, and don't think for one moment they would not. And how, Chloe, could I have gone out and fought in the battlefield if I had a wife at home? If I had loved what was in my household more than I loved my people?"

"You would be a man, rather than a machine," she said, bitterness in her words.

"I could not afford it."

"How can you afford this?" she asked.

"It is my life. It is my purpose."

"Damn your purpose," she said. "What about what you want?" She scrambled away from him, moving into a sitting position. "What about you?"

"I don't matter."

"You do! Sayid, you do."

"I can't," he bit out.

"Your uncle was a bastard. And he was wrong. Do you know what? I'm stronger now that I love Aden. I was weak when I didn't care. When I buried my head in books and cut my feelings off from everything. I had goals in my mind, and I even imagined I was passionate about them, but they were nothing compared to the love I feel for him. Nothing compared to the depth I've found in life, in myself, since his birth."

"That's good for you, Chloe, but it isn't meant for me."

She turned away from him and started collecting her clothes.

"Chloe," he said, his voice harsh, "your back…"

"What?" She reached around and felt raised welts across her skin. "Oh, from the rock."

"I hurt you," he said, his voice tortured.

"You didn't."

"I did."

"Sayid, it's fine."

"It's not fine," he roared. "This is what you would take from me? Pain? Perhaps you truly are like your mother. And perhaps I am the monster." He stood and tugged his pants on.

"Don't say that. It's demeaning to us both."

"But it is close to the truth, I think."

She shook her head. "It's not. You didn't hurt me on purpose."

"But someday, I will cause you pain, and whether

or not it happens by my hand, or by the hand of someone else, it is certain. And what you get in return will never match the risk. Because this, sex, this is all you will ever have from me."

"It wasn't just sex."

"Listen to yourself," he shouted. "Listen," he said again, his voice lowering. "You know nothing of men, nothing of relationships. You know labs and theory. This is no theory, this is a certainty. I can give you nothing. I want to give you nothing. This," he said, indicating her body, the wounds on her back, she imagined, "is all you will ever have from me."

"That's a lie, Sayid, and we both know it. You aren't protecting me right now. You're protecting you."

"And you want to see what is not there." He wrapped his hand around her wrist and pressed her palm to his chest. "There is nothing here," he spat. "Not anymore. Not for you."

He released his hold on her and turned and walked away, leaving her standing on the beach, naked, clutching her dress to her chest.

She would have given into the despair building inside of her, would have sank to the ground and wallowed in anguish. If she believed him.

If she hadn't glimpsed the fear and desperation in his eyes that proved that he felt no less than any other man. In some ways, it seemed he felt more. But it was locked down so deep, a well of it inside of him that was ready to overflow.

What she saw was a man drowning in his own body. And unless she reached in to save him, no one would.

CHAPTER THIRTEEN

STRATEGY WAS EVERYTHING. Knowing Sayid had taught Chloe that. It was the way he lived his life, the way he taught himself to survive. Sayid's strategy was to lie. To the world, and to himself.

And Chloe's strategy was to make it so he couldn't anymore. She'd given him a couple of days to cool off, had allowed him to avoid her, but now she was ready to make her move. While his defenses were down. And they were down. It was why he'd been so desperate to drive her away, she was certain of that.

"Hello, Sayid," she said, sweeping into the dining room, Aden in her arms.

Sayid was sitting at the head of the table, a computer in front of him along with his dinner. "Chloe. I wasn't expecting you," he said, his voice tight.

"Oh, you mean because last time we spoke you were an insulting bastard who accused me of being like my mother, after you had blistering sex on the beach with me? Yeah, I can see why you weren't expecting me for dinner. But Aden and I are joining you. Aren't you lucky?"

"Lucky wasn't the word I was looking for."

"Are you sure? Perhaps your English is faltering."

"I don't think it is, Chloe."

"Ah, well. I was studying today and I found out some really interesting things about Quantum Mechanics and a possible relationship to...do you think I could get some dinner?"

Sayid arched a brow but didn't say a word as he pressed a button beneath the table and paged a member of the staff who showed up promptly, taking Sayid's swift order for another place setting and going off to fulfill it.

"Thank you," she said, smiling sweetly.

"You're welcome," he returned, his tone bland.

"For a man who claims to have no emotion, you seem quite bothered by my presence."

"I'm not bothered by you."

"Oh. Could have fooled me." Her dinner, pheasant with a side of quinoa and steamed vegetables arrived quickly. "Thank you," she said to the server, then turned her focus back to Sayid. "What did you do today?"

"Small talk?"

"How else do two people get to know each other?"

"They can screw on the beach. That seemed to work pretty well."

Her cheeks heated. "Stop that."

"What?"

"Stop trying to scare me away with your macho man crap."

"I'm not trying to scare you away, I'm just not going to sugarcoat anything for your comfort."

She looked down at her dinner and pushed the quinoa around with her fork. She shifted Aden in her arms, then looked at Sayid. "Can you hold him? I want to eat."

"Where is his nanny?"

"I gave her the day off."

"Why did you do that?"

For this very reason. "Everyone needs a day off."

"I'm certain he would be fine if you set him down."

"What does it matter to you if you hold him for a moment, Sayid?" She was issuing a challenge now. If he truly felt nothing, not fear, not love, then holding Aden wouldn't affect him. But she knew it would. And she suspected he did, too.

"Give him to me," he said, his tone hard.

He knew how much she loved Aden, how much he meant to her. That she had set everything in her life, everything she'd cared about before, aside to be with him.

There was no greater show of trust in him than this, and he would know it.

She was also certain he would feel it. His loss was one he still felt deeply, and she didn't want to hurt him. But she did want him healed.

She crossed the room, cradling Aden close to her chest before holding him out to Sayid. "Support his head," she said, transferring him carefully into Sayid's strong arms.

Sayid looked up at her, his expression hard. Too hard. He was hiding behind his walls. Trying to feel nothing. Because he felt so much. Because he didn't want it used against him, ever again.

She knew now. She was certain.

"Aw, he didn't even cry. He knows his uncle."

Sayid's entire frame was stiff, but he held Aden, close to his chest, his large hands gentle on the baby's tiny body.

She backed up, sat in her chair, keeping one eye on Sayid and Aden as she ate. She let the silence stretch out, let Sayid feel the impact of holding him. Sayid was looking down at Aden, his expression fierce, the protectiveness, the vulnerability, on his face stunned her.

And then, in a moment it was gone, replaced with that hardness she was more accustomed to. Sayid looked away from Aden, his eyes fixed on the wall in front of him. Because he did feel. She knew he did.

"Have you nearly finished?" he asked a moment later, his voice clipped.

"Nearly," she responded.

"I have work to do, Chloe."

"And I have eating to do."

"I am a busy man, I'm the sheikh for all intents and purposes and I believe that takes precedence over you making sure you get a dinner that's easy to eat. Call the nanny if it's an emergency."

He stood and walked over to her chair, depositing Aden in her arms and striding from the room. And all Chloe could do was sit there and stare after him.

Sayid was choking again. What had she done to him? What had the baby done to him?

He'd been holding Aden, and doing just fine, but then he'd looked at him, looked right into his blue eyes, and he had felt a tug in his soul that had echoed through his entire being.

Panic had followed, a panic he couldn't understand or stop. It was still clawing at him, squeezing his throat, icy fingers wrapped around his neck. Pain. Pain from the past, what might have been, and a new pain, one borne of fresh desire, for things that were so near and yet still beyond him.

He had been avoiding her since that night on the beach, since he'd bared himself to her as he'd done. Told her about Sura. Lost all of his control.

Hurt her. Physically. Emotionally.

It had been a moment of freedom, being in her arms. A quiet moment when he'd felt one with himself. But the payment demanded for it had been swift and severe. The evidence of what he'd done to her with his loss of reserve.

But not just that. The evidence of how quickly the years of conditioning could be undone, all because of a woman. Because of Chloe.

And he had run from it. He'd tried to keep her from following by scaring her. Scaring her with the truth. Only she'd followed. She hadn't given up. His Chloe was stubborn. Stubborn and so very brave.

Part of him wanted to hold her to him. To have her. Possess her.

But there was the part of him, the part that still possessed humanity, that knew he couldn't. Knew he would give her nothing. He would try, endlessly, to fill himself with her, with her life, her light. And he would steal it all from her, giving nothing back.

"Sayid?" Chloe appeared in the doorway of his room.

"What are you doing here, Chloe?"

"I put Aden down for the night and I figured I'd come and see what the hell your problem is. Is that okay?"

"No. It's not. Go away."

"Why? Because I'm good enough to screw on the beach, but not good enough to talk to?"

"We talked already," he said.

"No. You talked. You told me what I felt, what I thought, who I was. And you were wrong, about all of it. So now I'm going to talk, and I'm going to tell you about you."

"Go," he bit out. "Go now, Chloe."

"No. Sayid, you think you can't feel? You're a liar. You feel. You feel when you touch me. You feel when you hold Aden. You feel right now. You're afraid. I know you are."

"You think you know what's going on inside of me, Chloe? You don't even want to know. You think you've seen darkness? You haven't seen what I've seen. You haven't done what I've done. I have killed men, Chloe, with my bare hands when necessary. And I've done it without remorse or regret, because it was for my country, for my people. The only way I could do that was by letting go."

"Everybody feels something, Sayid. Even a sociopath feels satisfaction in the deeds he commits, so don't try and tell me you simply feel nothing."

"All right, Chloe, all right, is this what you want to do? You want to share? You want me to share with you?"

She crossed her arms beneath her breasts. "Yes."

He nodded once. "You're right. I do feel. I feel one thing. Do you want to know what it is?"

She met his eyes, her expression determined. "Tell me."

"I'm angry. All the time." He hadn't realized it until he'd said it. "At everything, everyone. At life. At the lot I was given. I feed it, and it keeps me going. It's worse than nothing, because it consumes everything beautiful in life. Anger devours everything else, because happiness can't exist with it. Love cannot exist with it."

"And the day you lost Sura, and the future you imagined with her, you decided to be angry rather than be in pain. I understand that. But shouldn't you let it go?"

"You think this is about Sura? About the baby? I let it go long ago. I had to. But the lesson remains."

"You feel more than that, I know you do."

"I won't allow it," he bit out. "I can't."

"Why?"

"It isn't about what I want, it never has been. It's about Attar. It's about protecting my people, at the expense of myself. There is no other way. You serve yourself, or you serve others, but you cannot do both."

"I don't believe it. It's not about your people, it's about protecting you. That's all it's ever been about. Because you tasted loss, hideous, unspeakable loss, and you decided you would never experience it again."

"You think me a coward?"

"No more than the rest of us, Sayid. That's what I did. That's why I wouldn't have a relationship. Because I was too afraid of myself, of men. Too afraid to take a chance and simply trust myself or the people in my life. I hid behind my pain because it was easier than getting over it. Because it was safer. But I'm not safe. Admit it. That's why you have to push me away, because you feel for me."

"I don't," he growled.

"You do. If you didn't then you could just go about your business. You could sleep with me without worrying about what I felt, without trying to scare me off. If you were a machine, then you wouldn't care, but you do. You were given no more control in your life than I was, Sayid. Your uncle controlled you. He stole everything from you. He stole love, and happiness, and everything good, and he told you that you couldn't have it. And when you were a boy, there was nothing you could do. Why would you argue when it was the reality you were given? But you're a man now. Stand up and take it back. Take back what he took from you."

"No. I will never be weak like that. Not again."

"You think this is strength? Standing in the darkness, hiding yourself from the things in life that are real? From a nephew who would love you? Who would see you as his father? From the woman who loves you?"

"Chloe," he bit out, pain assaulting him, "don't."

She shook her head. "No. I'm not afraid anymore. I'm not afraid of being hurt. I don't want to be, but I'm not hiding. I love you, Sayid."

Everything in him wanted to pull her close to him, to take that love and fill himself with it. To turn the light on in his soul, her light, and fill all the dark corners with it.

To what end? To keep her until he drained her of the love she felt? Until she realized that she was wrong? That he couldn't give what she thought he could?

Never. He would never do that to her. To her or to Aden.

"Don't love me, Chloe."

"It's too late. And now you have to make a choice. Make a choice instead of simply accepting what life has given to you."

"You think me passive? I'm a warrior."

"Because it's easier for you," she said, her tone soft, steady. "Because it's easier for you to go out and fight than to let yourself care."

"I don't want to care. I don't care. And I don't want your love."

She drew back, as if he'd struck her, tears glistening in her blue eyes. "Coward," she whispered, a tear sliding down her cheek, one she didn't wipe away.

"Dammit, Chloe, how do you not understand? Men died because of me, because I couldn't keep myself from acting with my heart. Sura...the pain she was put through, all because she loved me. That's what happens when I feel, when I allow myself even one moment of escape from the hell I live in inside my own body. I cannot ever do it again. Not for you. Not for anyone. I'm going back to the city tomorrow," he said. "You and Aden are welcome to stay on here for a while. It is quieter."

"You mean you're keeping me here," she said.

"For a while."

"Tell me you don't love me, Sayid."

He met her eyes, ignoring the burning in his chest, ignoring the clawing sense of suffocation. "I don't love you."

Another tear slid down her cheek, and in that moment, he would have gladly put his back to a whip and taken its blows. Anything other than facing her now. Than lying like this.

But it was for her. For both of them.

For Attar.

An ideal cannot fail.

She lifted her chin, her voice steady. "Then Aden and I will stay here for a while. Please have my whiteboards and books sent over."

"I will."

She turned away from him and he saw a tremor go through her body. "Sayid," she said, without facing him again, "you taught me to take control of myself, of what I want, and for that, I can only thank you. I wish I could have helped you too. I wish I could have taken your burdens. Just for a while."

She started to walk away, and he couldn't stop the words that came spilling out of his mouth. "But my burdens aren't yours to carry, *habibti,* and they never will be." It was the kindest thing for her. The only thing. They would crush her, even as they were crushing him.

She did turn then. "But you took mine. How could I do anything less?"

"You will never have to know."

She nodded once, then walked out of the room. He watched the place where she had been, the man inside of him clawing at his chest, begging to be let out. Begging to be allowed to go after her.

And the darkness swallowed him whole.

Chloe's tears fell onto her whiteboard, running down the surface, smudging her equation. She didn't care. Not then. There was no reasoning her way out of this.

She'd been so sure that she wasn't even trying. That she was feeling, and not reasoning, but that was a lie. She'd been trying to reason out Sayid, to make him make sense in her mind, to make his problems something that she could solve so that she could have him to herself.

So that she could make him love her.

She blinked, trying to stop a fresh onslaught of tears from falling. She'd been trying to make him palatable. Make him the man she wished he could be, rather than the man that he was.

That was something her mother would do. It was something she'd always done. Put blind spots over her father's sins, seeing only the good, singing his praises with a split lip that had been injured at his hand.

So she'd been afraid to do the same. Afraid to simply want Sayid as he was.

But there was a difference between Sayid and her father. Her father turned his anger outward, hurting everyone around him, taking nothing on himself.

While Sayid turned it inward, and let it burn him alive.

She'd meant to save him. Meant to show him what he could have. What they could have.

You wanted to show him the future you wanted for him.

That stopped her cold, made her heart freeze. "Oh…Sayid," she whispered.

She had done to him what people had done to him

all of his life. She'd tried to make him her ideal. Had tried to tell him what he should want, had tried to force him to want what she wanted.

That wasn't love. That was selfishness. Possessiveness. She'd tried to own him, as she'd done their first night together, his hands bound, his body at her mercy.

She'd tried to make him belong to her, to be the man that she needed. And she hadn't tried, not truly, to be the woman that he needed. Because she'd ignored everything he'd said he felt, dismissed it as a lie. Had told him it didn't have to be that way and that he could have other things, without ever truly listening to what he did want.

She'd been no better than the others who'd tried to trap him. Who'd tried to manipulate him. As his uncle had done, stealing the woman he loved, robbing him of his child. His future. So that he could harness Sayid.

And she'd tried to do the same. Tried to tame him, make him a man she could handle.

She wiped her hand over everything on her whiteboard, smearing it past the point of being readable, and forked her fingers through her hair. No wonder he had turned her away. She'd made herself think she was making an offer, when all she was making was demands.

She turned and walked out of her makeshift study and ran down the halls, toward Sayid's office.

"Curse this massive castle," she panted as she took

the second flight of stairs on her way to his personal quarters.

She ran down the long corridor and wrenched the door open. The room was empty. She turned around, panic clawing at her, before she started out of the room, down the hall. She ran into one of Sayid's men.

"Where is the sheikh?" she asked, knowing she sounded as shaky and emotional as she felt, not caring.

"The sheikh left. He went back to the capital city."

"When?"

"A couple of hours ago."

"How?"

"I'm sorry?"

"Did he take a helicopter? Did he walk? Magic carpet?"

"The helicopter I believe."

She swore and turned back for his office. She walked over to his phone and punched the button that would put her through to the palace. It was answered by one of the office staff.

"Is Sheikh Sayid in?"

"Who is calling?"

"His wife," she said.

"I'm sorry, sheikha, but he isn't in."

She slammed the phone down and planted her palms on the desk, despair covering her like a blanket. And then she saw a name on the speed dial that sent prickles over her skin.

She picked the handset up again, and punched the number.

"Sayid?" The voice on the other end was deep, the Russian accent thick.

"Vasin," she said.

"Not Sayid. Sheikha?"

"Yes. And I seem to be missing my husband. You found him once, and I need you to find him again."

"I can do that."

Sayid ran across the desert sand, his entire body burning with anguish, a pain that had no name, and no way of being stopped.

He had run out into the desert countless times, hoping to somehow find a moment of release, a moment of freedom. A moment to himself.

He had only ever found it in Chloe's arms. Had only ever truly been free when he was bound to her, for her.

And she had not used his weakness against him. She was the only one. The only one who had not taken his emotion and used it to exploit him.

The only one who never would.

And he had told her he didn't want her. He had told her he didn't love her.

And she had called him a coward. She was right. He had spent so long hiding in anger. Anger had been safe, anger had sustained him. So much so that he had started to believe it was nothing. That he had ceased to feel it.

He had wanted to scream into the emptiness of the desert so many times. Had wanted to release the pain, the pressure, had wanted to tear out of his body, his prison, and let the man he was inside run free. But pain was not acceptable. Showing pain would expose him.

But it didn't mean it wasn't there. Eating him alive as he screamed inside.

Always, always he had been too tightly wrapped in the chains Kalid had put around him to do it.

But the break of losing Chloe had loosened the chains, had put a crack in the defenses. He fought against it, fought against the darkness that threatened to pull him back down.

And he thought of Chloe's face.

He fell to his knees and let out the roar that had been building inside of him for more than half of his life. He let it all flow through him, the pain of being whipped by Kalid. The indignity, the shame, the overwhelming pain of captivity at the hands of his enemies.

The loss of Sura. The loss she'd endured on his behalf. So great, so profound, it brought tears to his eyes. And he let them fall. Let it all pour from him for the first time. For the first time, he grieved rather than hiding.

And when he was through, he stood. And the walls inside were gone.

* * *

The phone on Sayid's desk rang, and Chloe answered it. "Hello?"

"Sheikha." It was Alik.

"Did you find him?"

"I did. But he is so close to you, I think you should simply wait a moment."

"What? Alik…what do you…?"

"Chloe."

She looked up and saw Sayid in the doorway. And she hung up the phone. "What are you doing here?"

"Alik contacted me, but I was already on my way back."

"It's been a week. Where have you been?"

"The desert," he said. "I had to…the desert is where I lost myself, I thought perhaps I might find myself there. Last place I left me, and all."

"And did you?"

He shook his head. "Not as you might think."

"I needed to find you."

"Didn't you already say all that could be said?"

"No. I didn't. I realized something after you left, Sayid. I realized that I was just doing to you what everyone has done to you all of your life. I was trying to make you right for me, trying to make you fit my expectation while I ignored what you said. What you wanted. I have to respect that even if it isn't what I want, who you are is valuable. And what you want is valuable. What you feel, or don't feel, is up to you, and it's personal. It's yours. Because you don't belong to a country, or even to me, you belong to you. No one has ever given you that respect, and I realize that I didn't either. You deserve better than that. From me. From everyone."

"Oh, Chloe." He walked toward her, rounding the desk, pulling her into his arms and tugging her against him. "Do you feel that?" he asked.

"What?"

He took her hand and placed it on his chest, his heart beat raging against her palm. "That. My heart."

"Yes," she whispered.

"Love. I feel it."

"Oh." She leaned in and kissed his chest. "Oh, Sayid." She rested her head there, just listening to the beat of his heart for a moment.

"Chloe," he said, sifting his fingers through her hair. "Don't you understand? I didn't find myself in the desert, because you weren't there. I found myself with you. And it frightened me. I didn't recognize the feeling, the fear, because it had been so long since I'd been allowed to feel it, but that's what it was."

She lifted her head so that she could look at him, could look into his eyes. They weren't flat now, they were shining.

"Do you know what I was afraid of, Chloe?"

"What?" she whispered.

"Not of enemies. Not like I thought. That's what I was told, why I was told I couldn't feel. But the simple truth is, the enemies of my people harmed my body, but it was Kalid who scarred my soul. Kalid who used my emotion against me. Everything that gave me happiness he saw taken from me. Everything I wanted, he held out of my reach. Every emotion I had he exposed as a weakness and he used it to bend me to his will. To make me into the man, into the thing, that he wanted. His personal super soldier. A machine who might as well have metal in his chest instead of a beating heart. Everyone I cared about has used my emotions against me, and with you, Chloe, I had no defenses."

"Oh, Sayid…"

"Do you know how badly I needed that?" he asked. "With you, I could be powerless, and you didn't use it against me. That first night, when you tied me to the bed…"

"At your request," she said.

"At my request," he said. "I found freedom in giving control to someone else. In letting go for a moment, of all the things, all of the conditioning I'd been subjected to. And then, on the beach…I was undone, Chloe. I couldn't handle what you made me feel."

"And I pushed you."

"I needed to be pushed. I thought…since I had to take over as ruler…I thought I was breaking. It wasn't me that was breaking. It was those walls, those damned walls that I've been trapped behind for most of my life."

"I was asking things of you that I shouldn't have.

I was asking you to be something I needed, instead of asking you what you needed."

"You," he said, his voice rough, "I needed you. I still do. I will, forever. Because I can be exposed to you. Because you set me free."

"I feel like all I've done is take things from you," she said. "You...you made me feel so safe. You let me bind your hands when you've been through that before in such awful circumstances. You married me so that I could have Aden. You...you've taken all my fear and my pain, you've given me something totally new. A fresh start, a new way to look at love."

"I'm so happy to hear you say that, *habibti,* because before you, there was a hole inside of me, and I was certain, certain that I must have stolen from you in order to fill it. Because I'm not empty anymore, Chloe."

"Maybe that's what love is supposed to be, Sayid. It doesn't take, it only adds more."

"I think you're right."

"I know that was my experience with Aden. As much as it cost me, and at first it felt like a cost, to have him, just loving him gave me back so much more."

Sayid took in a shuddering breath. "Aden," he said. "And you. It seems like far too much for a man like me to have. It seems so much more than I deserve."

"No, Sayid. It's everything you've always deserved, everything that was stolen from you."

"You make me believe it," he said. "You make me

feel…I have never felt like I was worth anything. I've never felt like my life mattered. But when I look into your eyes, I know that it does."

"It does," she whispered, pain, pain for all he had been through, constricting her throat. "You matter so much. Not because of what you can give the world, although you've given so much, and will always give more, but because of what you give to me. Because of what you'll give to Aden."

"I want…" his voice was husky, choked, "I want to be his father. To be your husband. To be your family."

A tear slipped down her cheek. "I want that, too."

"I love you, Chloe. With you, everything makes sense. With you, I don't feel like I'm trapped inside of myself. I just…am."

"And you've shown me that love gives, it gives more than it takes. As you've given to me."

"And as you've done for me."

"What do you think? Sixteen years of marriage doesn't seem so bad now, does it?" she asked, leaning in and kissing his lips.

"It still doesn't seem ideal."

She frowned. "It doesn't?"

"No, Chloe al Kadar, I don't want sixteen years. I want nothing less than a lifetime. You have to admit, since we love each other, it's the only logical thing."

"Well, Sheikh Sayid al Kadar, since you have presented me with completely infallible logic, I accept."

"So, in the end my logic won you over."

She shook her head. "No. In the end, it was your love that won."

A couple months later, they discovered that breast-feeding wasn't the world's most effective form of birth control.

Chloe sat on the edge of their bed, in their shared room, with a shocked look on her face.

"You're a scientist," Sayid said dryly, the distressed look on his wife's face nearly comical. "You should have known this could happen."

"Oh, shut up."

"You're hormonal already."

She picked up a pillow and threw it at him. "You aren't freaking out," she said.

"I'm not. Because I'm happy."

"You are?" she asked.

"Why wouldn't I be happy? This time with you and Aden…these have been the best months of my life. You were right about love," he said. "It just keeps growing, and now…now it's going to grow even more."

"This might be the second son," she said.

He nodded. "And he will be treated no different than the first. And the one after him will be treated no different. All of our children will be loved. And they will be here, with us."

She nodded, a smile on her lovely face. "Yes. That's what I want."

"You were afraid I would not?"

"Not really but…tradition…"

"Damn tradition. I already have you in my room, in my bed every night. Aden already spends more time with us than with his nannies. I have no interest in tradition. I want a family."

"That's all I've ever wanted."

"I'm so glad we get to have it together."

EPILOGUE

Sixteen years later...

"WHERE IS ADEN?"

Chloe turned at the sound of her husband's voice, nerves fluttering in her stomach. "He's in his room."

"And is he ready?"

"He's just a boy, Sayid."

"He's the heir to the throne of Attar. And he's about to take his place."

She nodded. "I know. He was born for it. He's spent his life preparing for it...but..."

"But you're his mother, and you can't help but worry about him." Sayid crossed the room and pulled her into his arms. Sixteen years hadn't diminished the power of his touch. To create desire in her body, to fill her with lust, with need. With love. "I'm his father. I feel the same way. But he's strong. He's smart. And he has us."

She nodded. "I know."

"Are the other children ready?"

"I'm just hoping no one spilled anything on their

clothes. They got dressed so early it doesn't seem like all the outfits will make it through to the coronation clean."

"It doesn't matter if they don't. We've never pretended to be a traditional royal family."

"I don't suppose we had a hope of it."

"No, Dr. al Kadar," Sayid said. "I don't suppose we did. Not many sheikhas teach at universities."

"And not many sheikhs have children's artwork hanging all over their office."

"I suppose not. But not many sheikhs have a family as wonderful as mine."

Aden appeared in the doorway, his clothing perfectly pressed, the expression on his young face fill with utter seriousness. A surge of pride, of love, went through Chloe. Her oldest son was a man now in the eyes of the country, but to her, he would always be the baby she'd cradled to her chest. The baby she'd give up everything for.

The baby that had, in the end, given her everything in her life that mattered.

"I'm ready," he said.

"So are we," Sayid said, keeping on arm around Chloe's waist and putting his hand on Aden's shoulder. "As soon as you want to go in, we'll follow."

"I'm glad you'll be with me," Aden said.

"Always. We're always here behind you."

"I've never doubted that." He gave them both a smile and walked back out, toward the throne room, toward his future.

"That boy," Sayid said, "is the hope of a nation. But more than that, he's our son. He brought us together. Nothing will change that."

"I know," Chloe said. She turned to Sayid and kissed him, kissed him with all of the passion that had built between them, grown, over the years of their marriage. "If we had kept to our original plan, this is the day we would have gone our separate ways."

Sayid wrapped his arms tightly around her and pulled her against him. "Instead, I think I'll hold on to you a little bit tighter."

She encircled his waist, pressing her hands to his lower back. "Me, too."

"Will you put on your glasses later and talk to me in your stern professor voice?"

She laughed. "If you don't behave yourself during this very solemn occasion, I may tie you to the bed." She kissed his lips again. "It will give you something to look forward to."

"Habibti, with you, I always have something to look forward to."

* * * * *